THE FLYING BEAVER BROTHERS AND THE CRAZY CRITTER RACE

MAXWELL EATON III

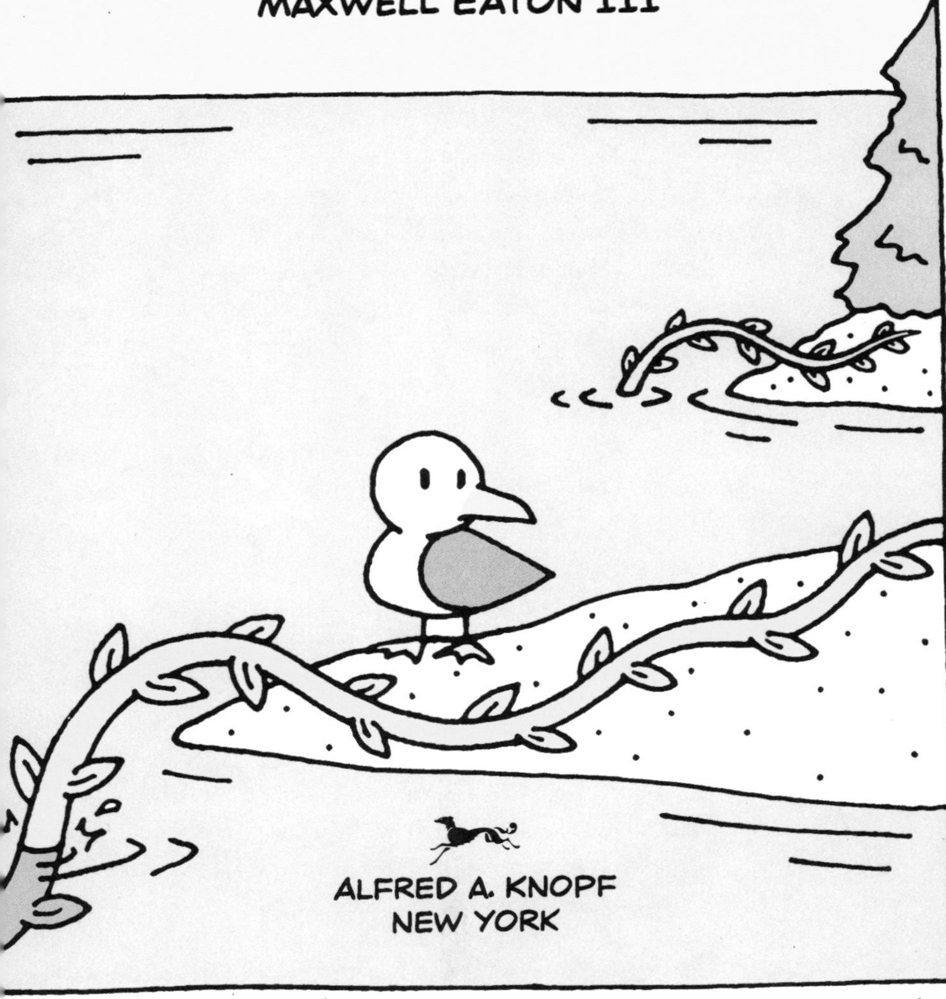

ALFRED A. KNOPF
NEW YORK

For KEE

THIS IS A BORZOI BOOK PUBLISHED BY ALFRED A. KNOPF

Visit us on the Web! randomhousekids.com
Educators and librarians, for a variety of teaching tools, visit us at RHTeachersLibrarians.com
Library of Congress Cataloging-in-Publication Data
Eaton, Maxwell.
The flying beaver brothers and the Crazy Critter Race / Maxwell Eaton III. — First edition.
p. cm. — (The flying beaver brothers ; 6)
Summary: When Ace and Bub compete in a race to win a new houseboat, they unwittingly plant fast-spreading vines instead of trees on the Shark Tooth Islands, forcing their inhabitants to live in the sea.
ISBN 978-0-385-75469-9 (trade) — ISBN 978-0-385-75470-5 (lib. bdg.) — ISBN 978-0-385-75471-2 (ebook)
1. Graphic novels. [1. Graphic novels. 2. Beavers—Fiction. 3. Islands—Fiction.
4. Climbing plants—Fiction. 5. Raccoons—Fiction.] I. Title.
PZ7.7.E18Flm 2014
741.5'973—dc23
2014019530
The illustrations were created using pen and ink with digital coloring.
MANUFACTURED IN MALAYSIA • March 2015 • 10 9 8 7 6 5 4 3 2 1 • First Edition

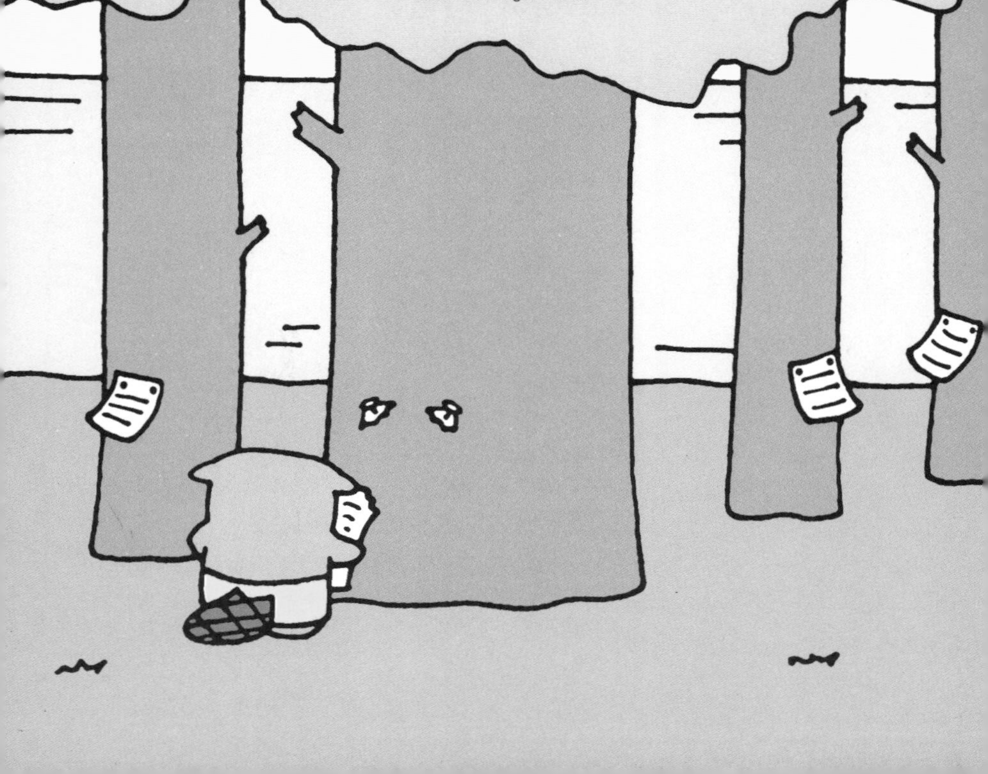

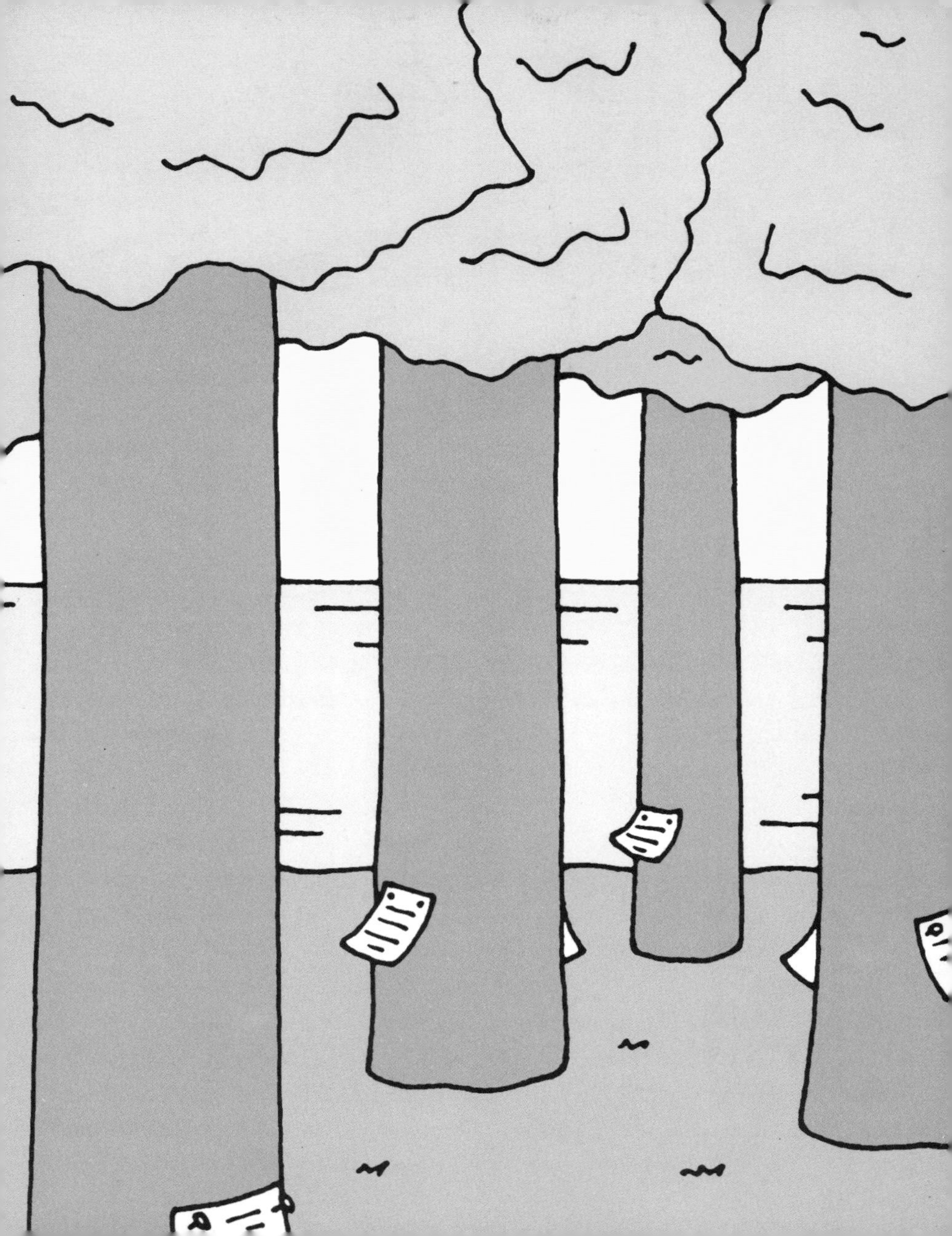

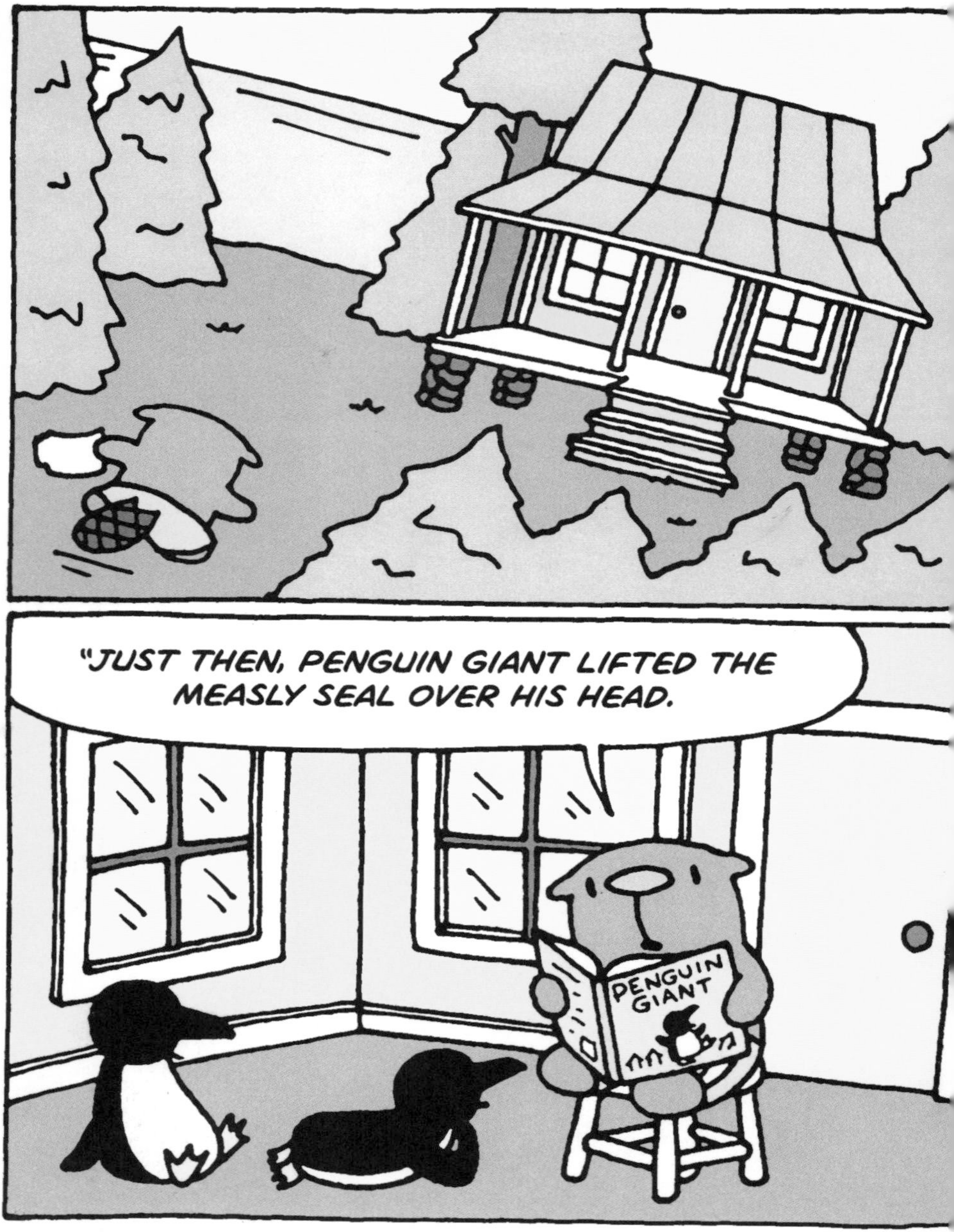
"JUST THEN, PENGUIN GIANT LIFTED THE MEASLY SEAL OVER HIS HEAD.
PENGUIN GIANT

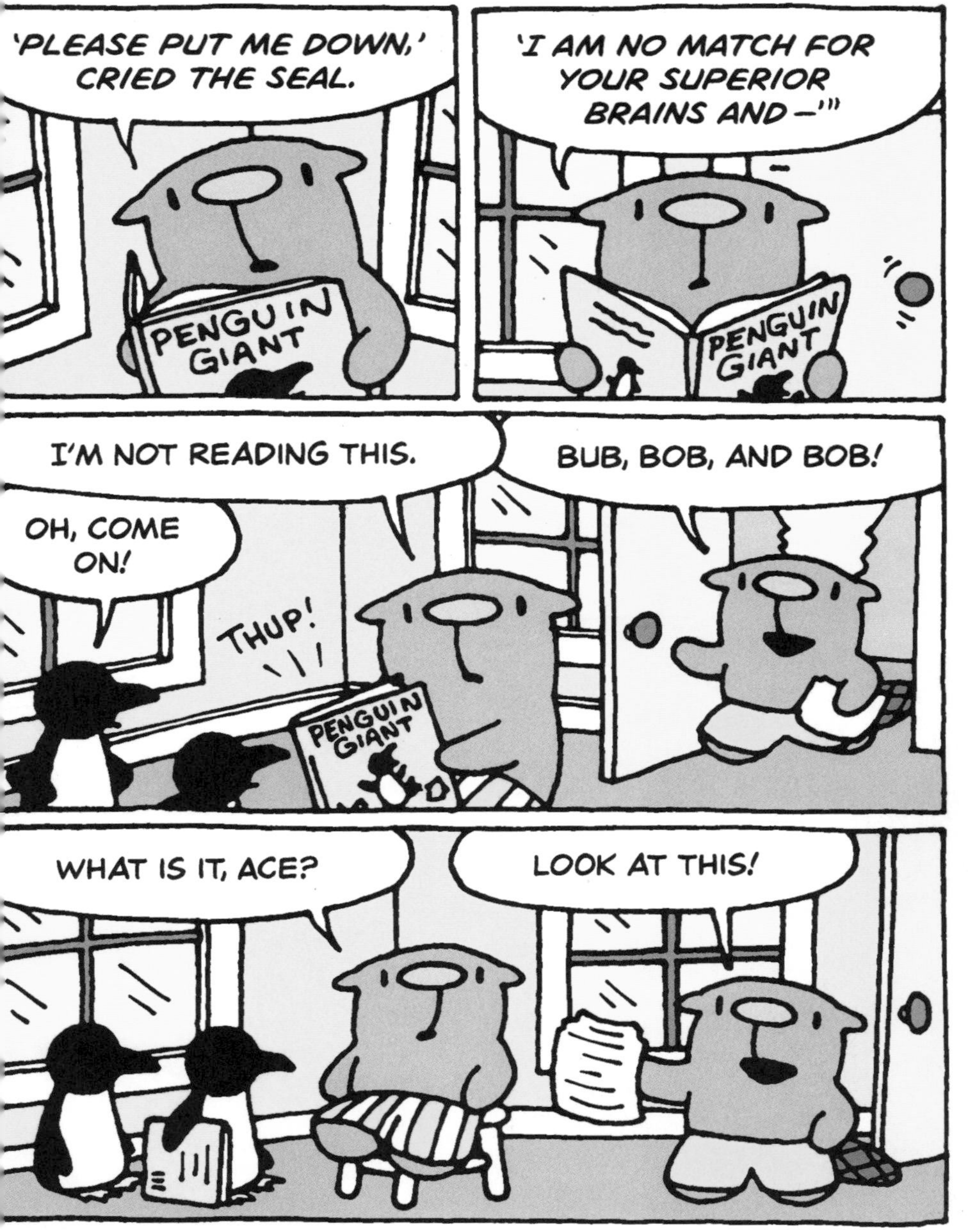
'PLEASE PUT ME DOWN,' CRIED THE SEAL.
PENGUIN GIANT
'I AM NO MATCH FOR YOUR SUPERIOR BRAINS AND—'"
PENGUIN GIANT
I'M NOT READING THIS.
OH, COME ON!
THUP!
PENGUIN GIANT
BUB, BOB, AND BOB!
WHAT IS IT, ACE?
LOOK AT THIS!

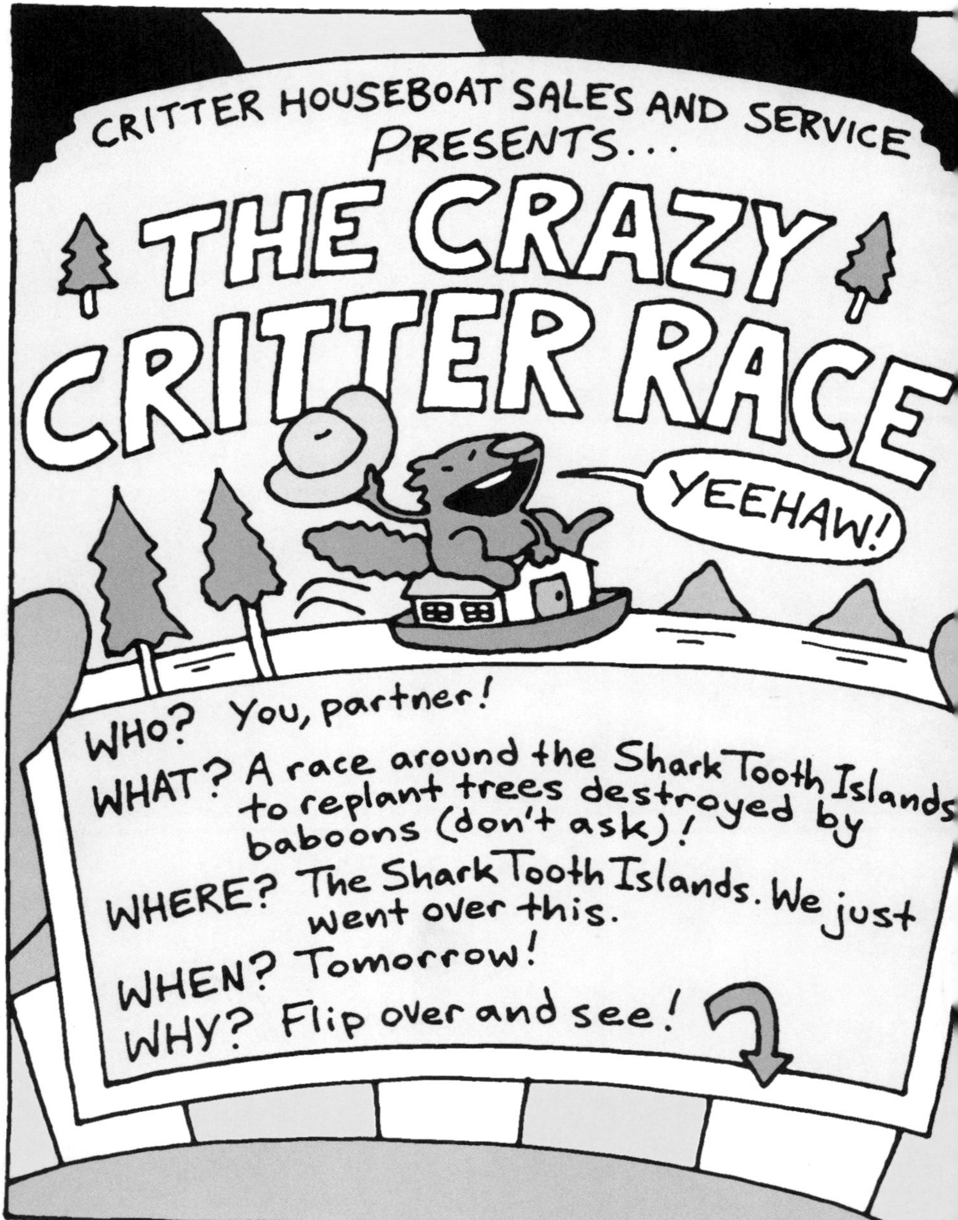
CRITTER HOUSEBOAT SALES AND SERVICE PRESENTS...
THE CRAZY CRITTER RACE
YEEHAW!
WHO? You, partner!
WHAT? A race around the Shark Tooth Islands to replant trees destroyed by baboons (don't ask)!
WHERE? The Shark Tooth Islands. We just went over this.
WHEN? Tomorrow!
WHY? Flip over and see!

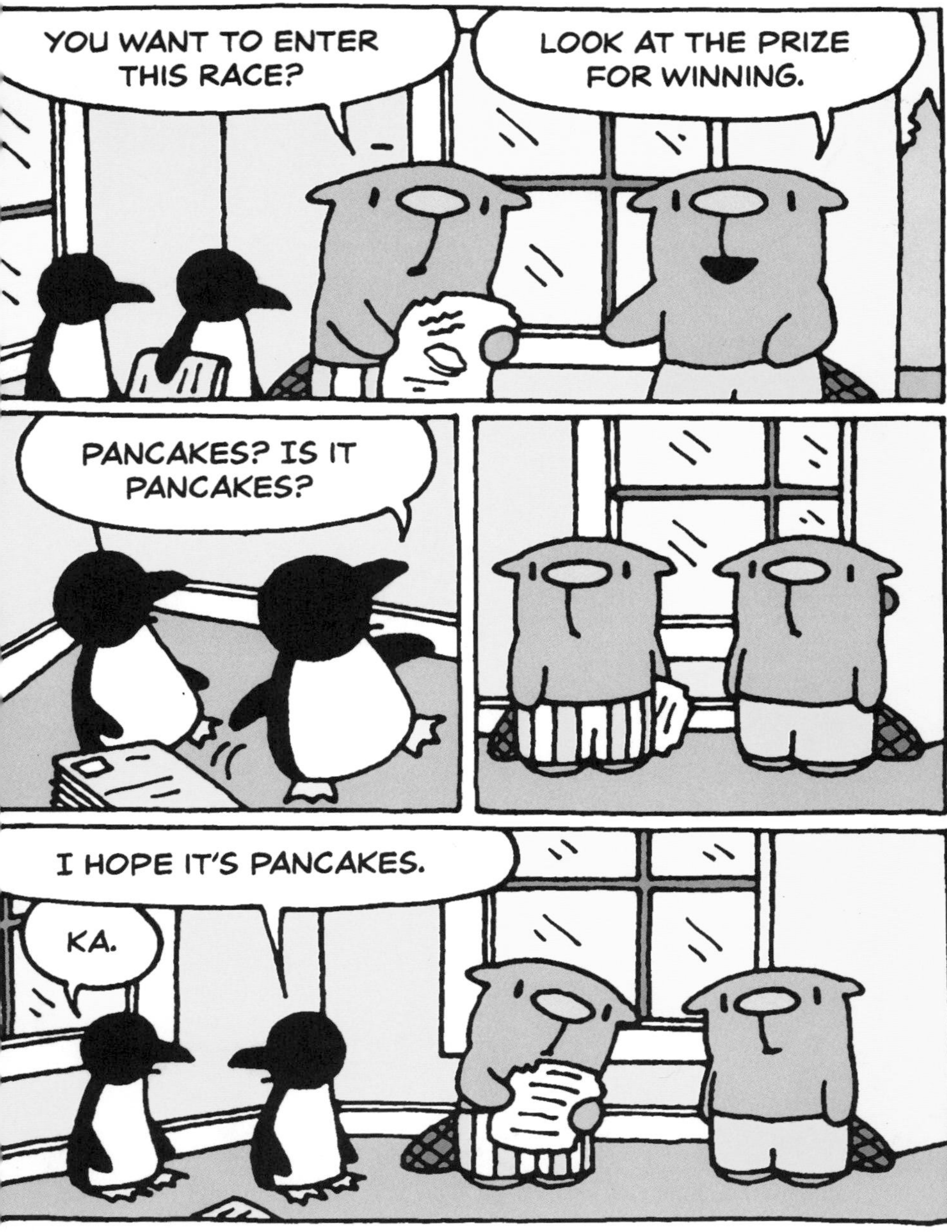
YOU WANT TO ENTER THIS RACE?
LOOK AT THE PRIZE FOR WINNING.
PANCAKES? IS IT PANCAKES?
I HOPE IT'S PANCAKES.
KA.

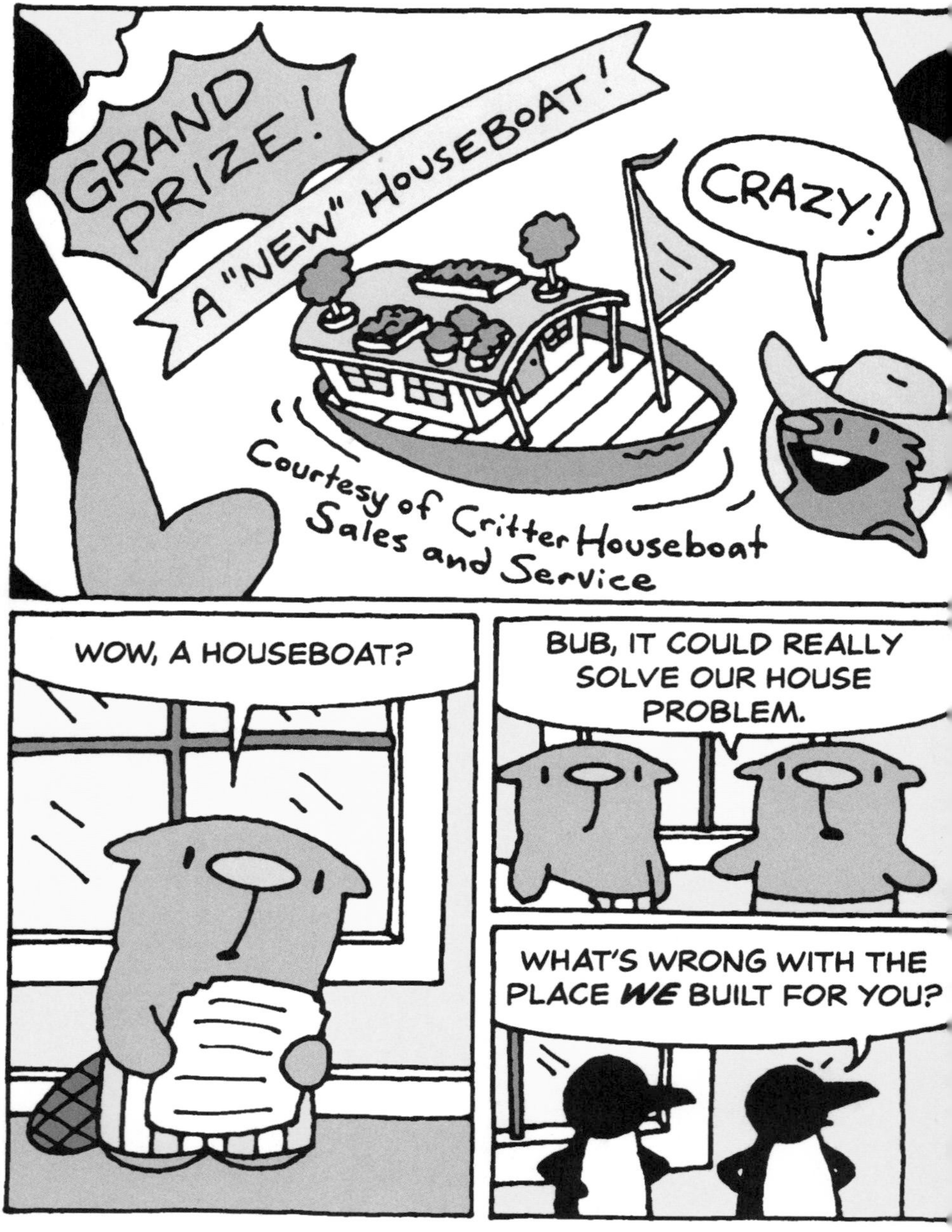
GRAND PRIZE!
A "NEW" HOUSEBOAT!
Courtesy of Critter Houseboat Sales and Service
CRAZY!
WOW, A HOUSEBOAT?
BUB, IT COULD REALLY SOLVE OUR HOUSE PROBLEM.
WHAT'S WRONG WITH THE PLACE *WE* BUILT FOR YOU?

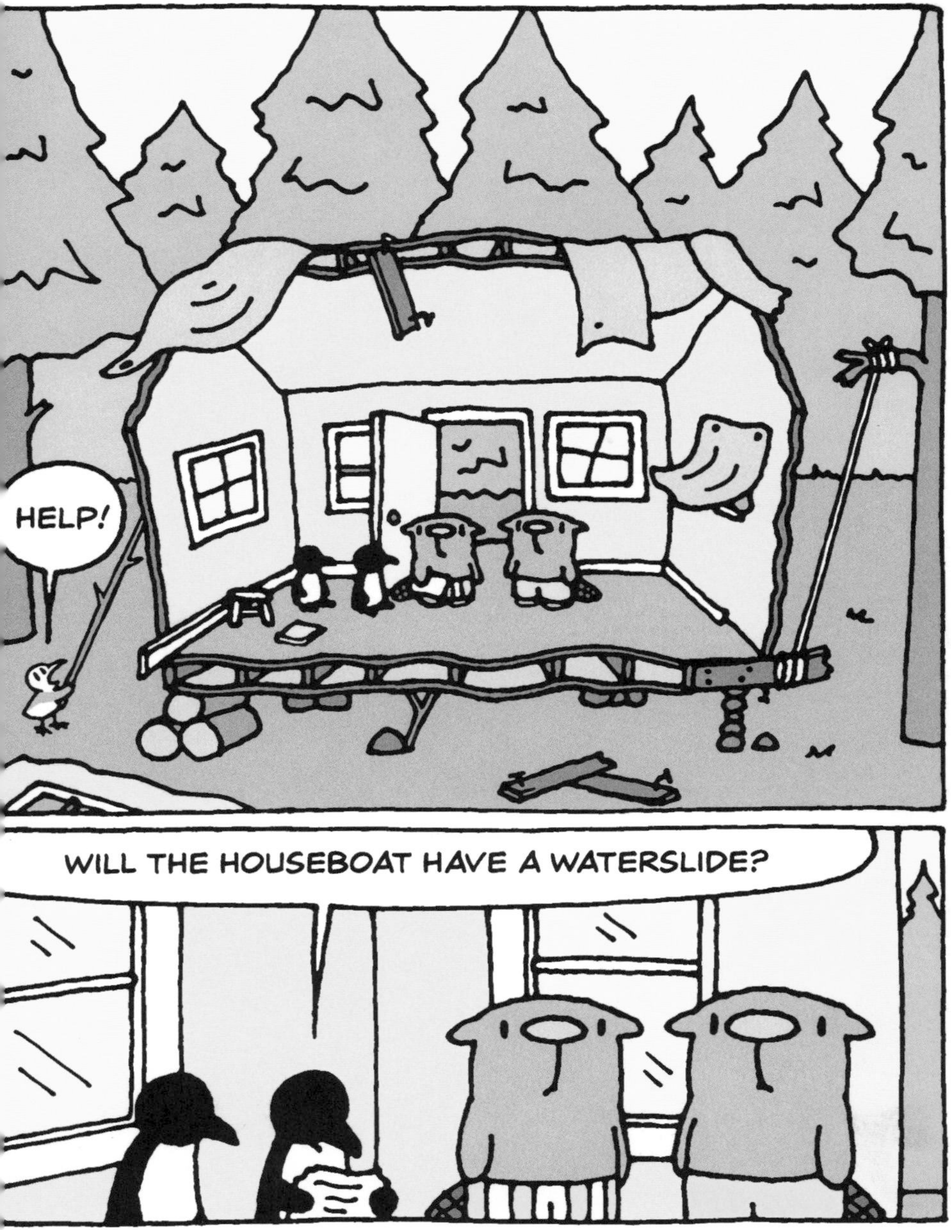
HELP!
WILL THE HOUSEBOAT HAVE A WATERSLIDE?

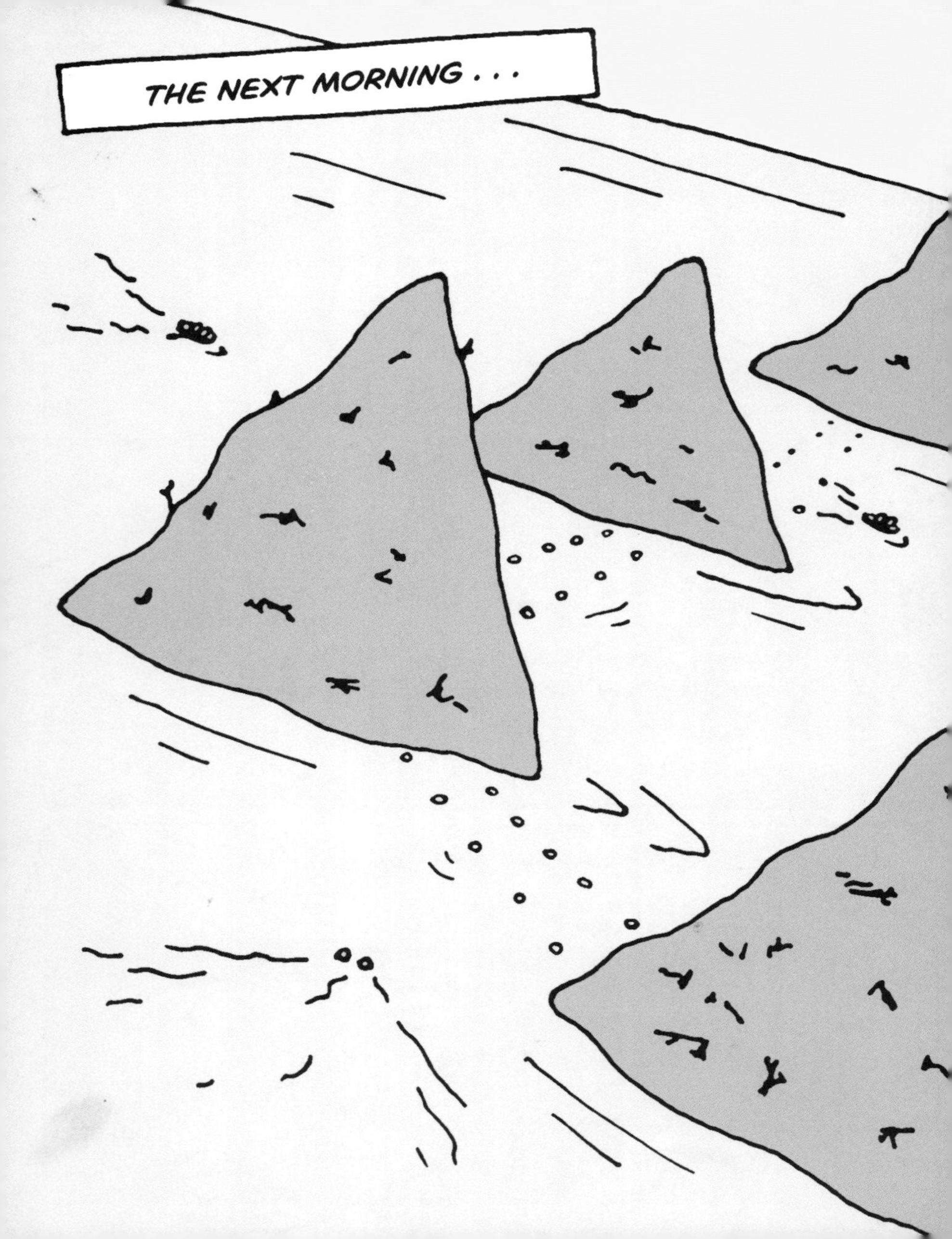
THE NEXT MORNING . . .

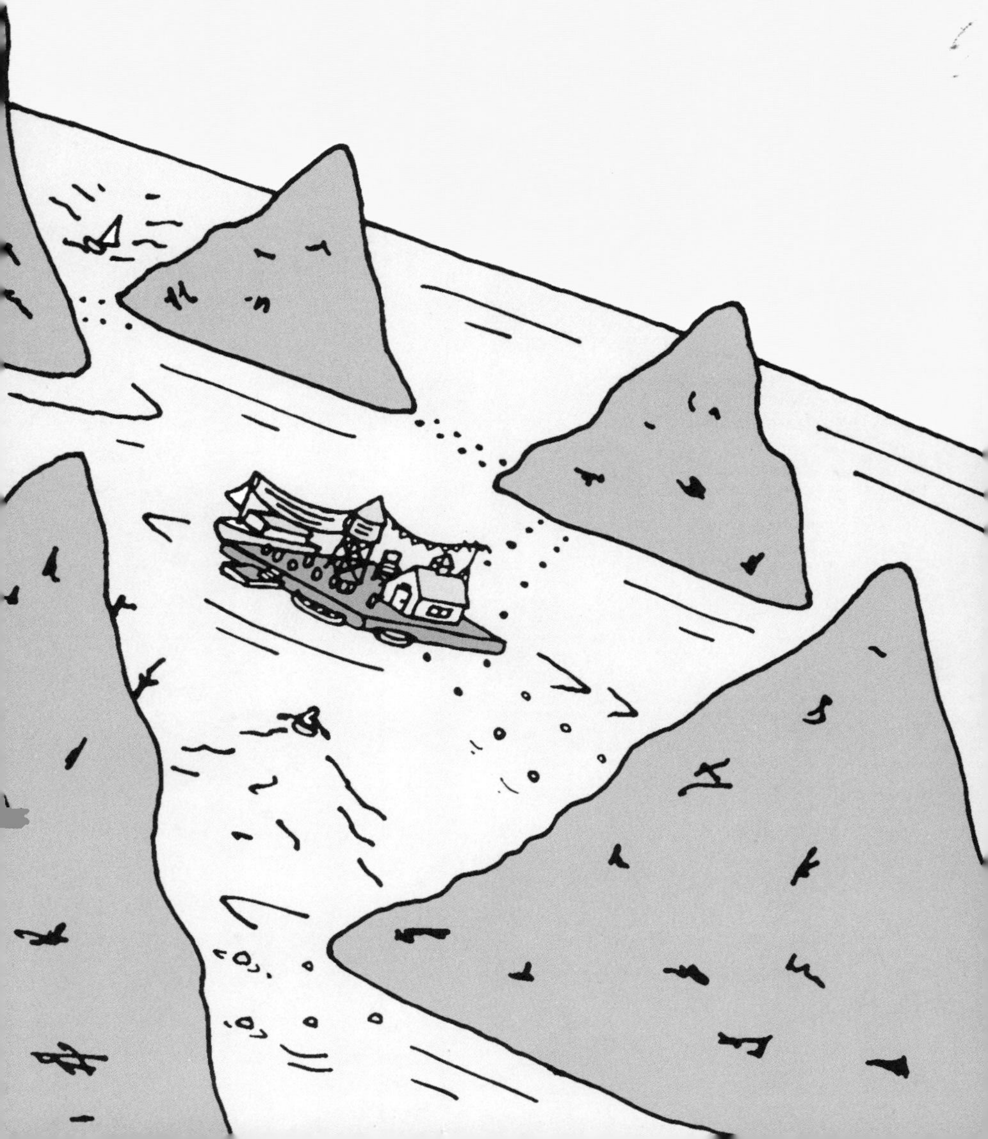

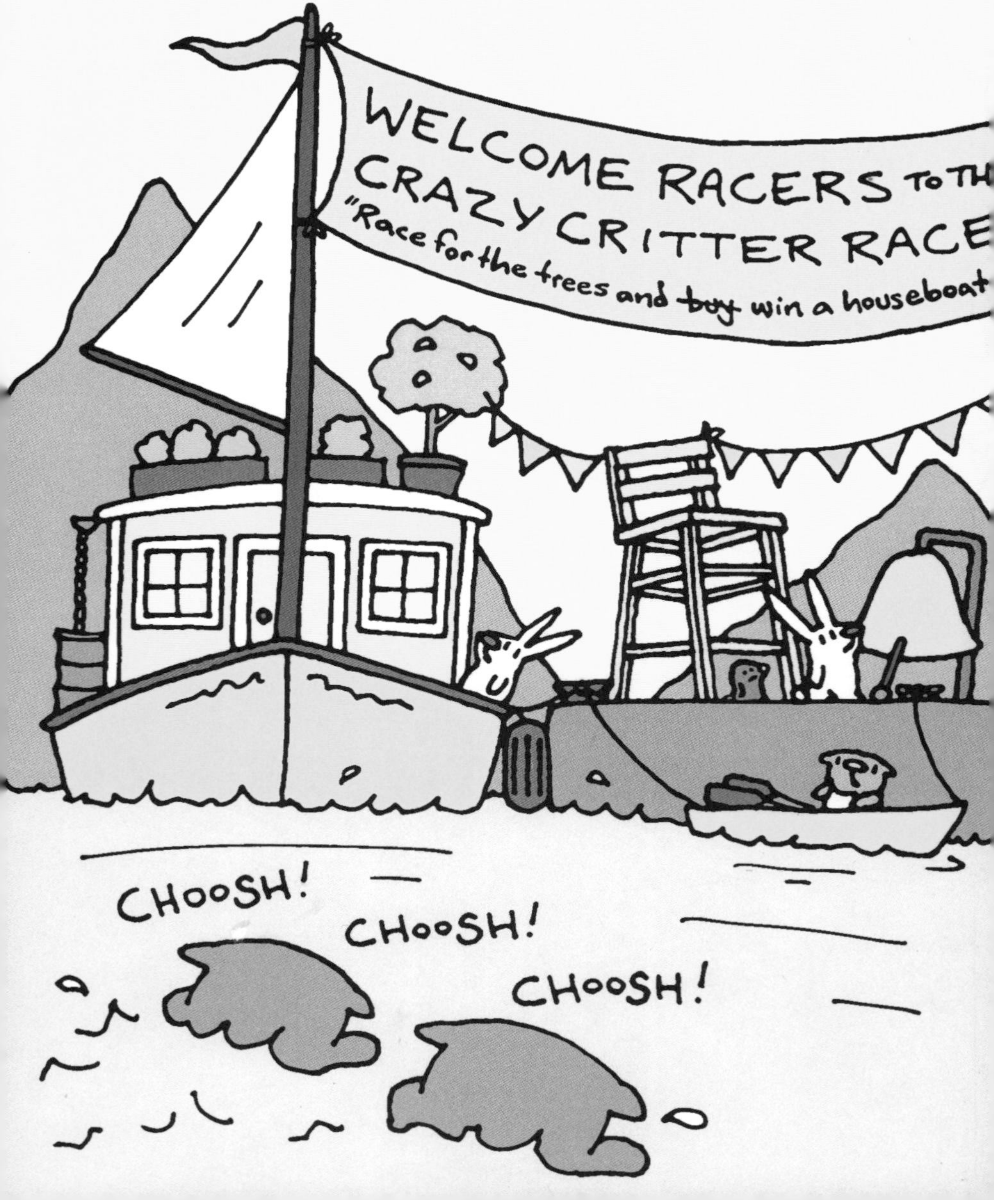
WELCOME RACERS TO TH
CRAZY CRITTER RACE
"Race for the trees and ~~buy~~ win a houseboat
CHOOSH!
CHOOSH!
CHOOSH!

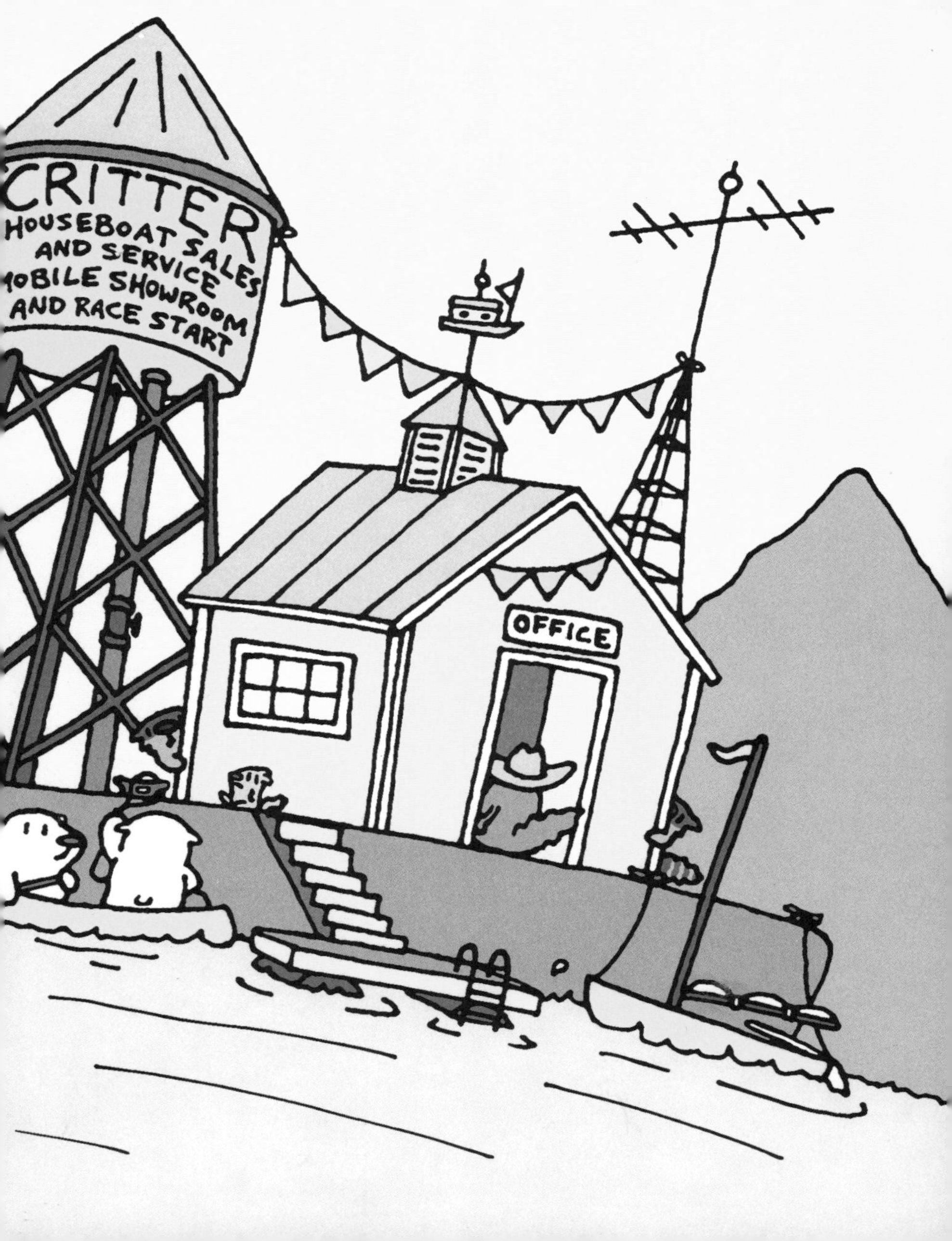
CRITTER
HOUSEBOAT SALES
AND SERVICE
MOBILE SHOWROOM
AND RACE START
OFFICE

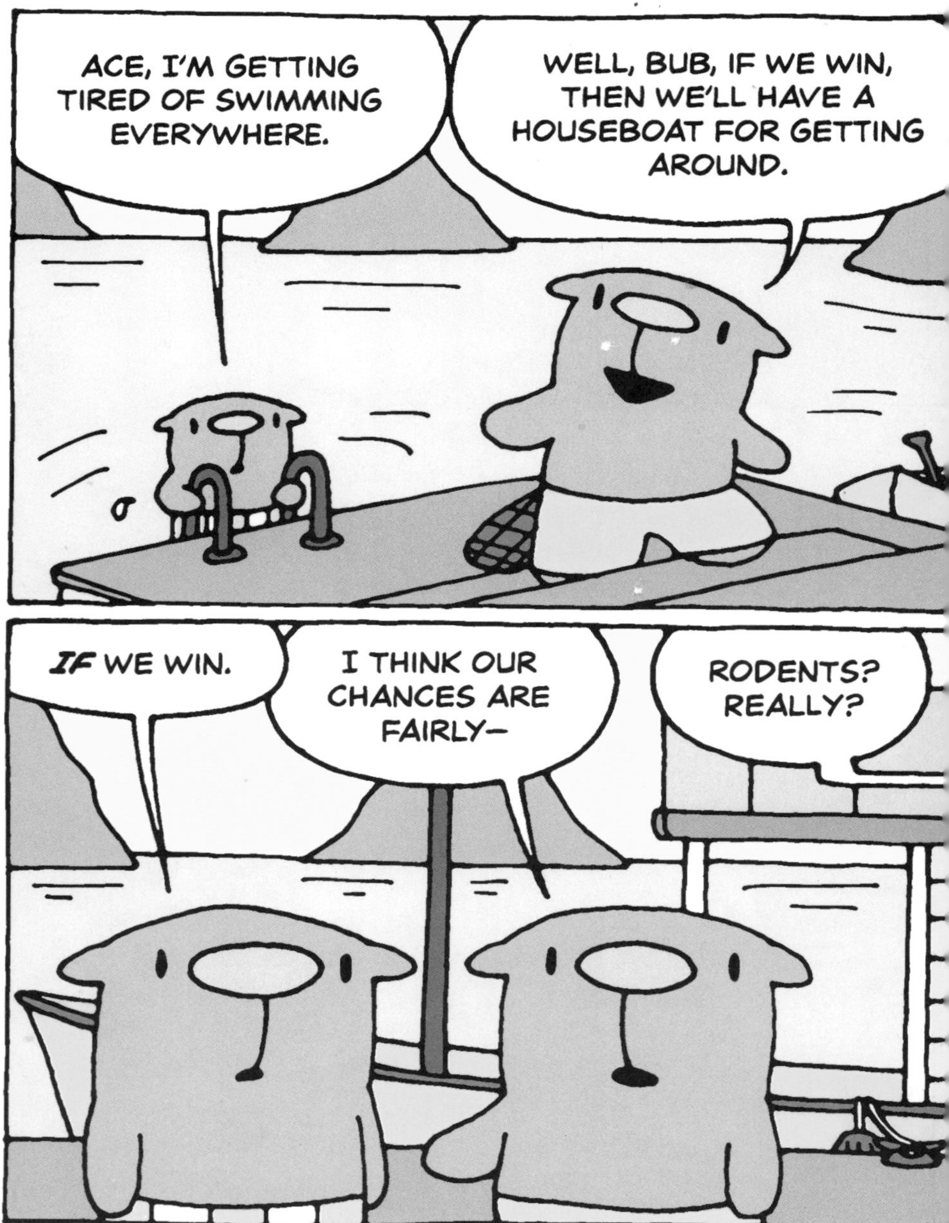
ACE, I'M GETTING TIRED OF SWIMMING EVERYWHERE.
WELL, BUB, IF WE WIN, THEN WE'LL HAVE A HOUSEBOAT FOR GETTING AROUND.
IF WE WIN.
I THINK OUR CHANCES ARE FAIRLY—
RODENTS? REALLY?

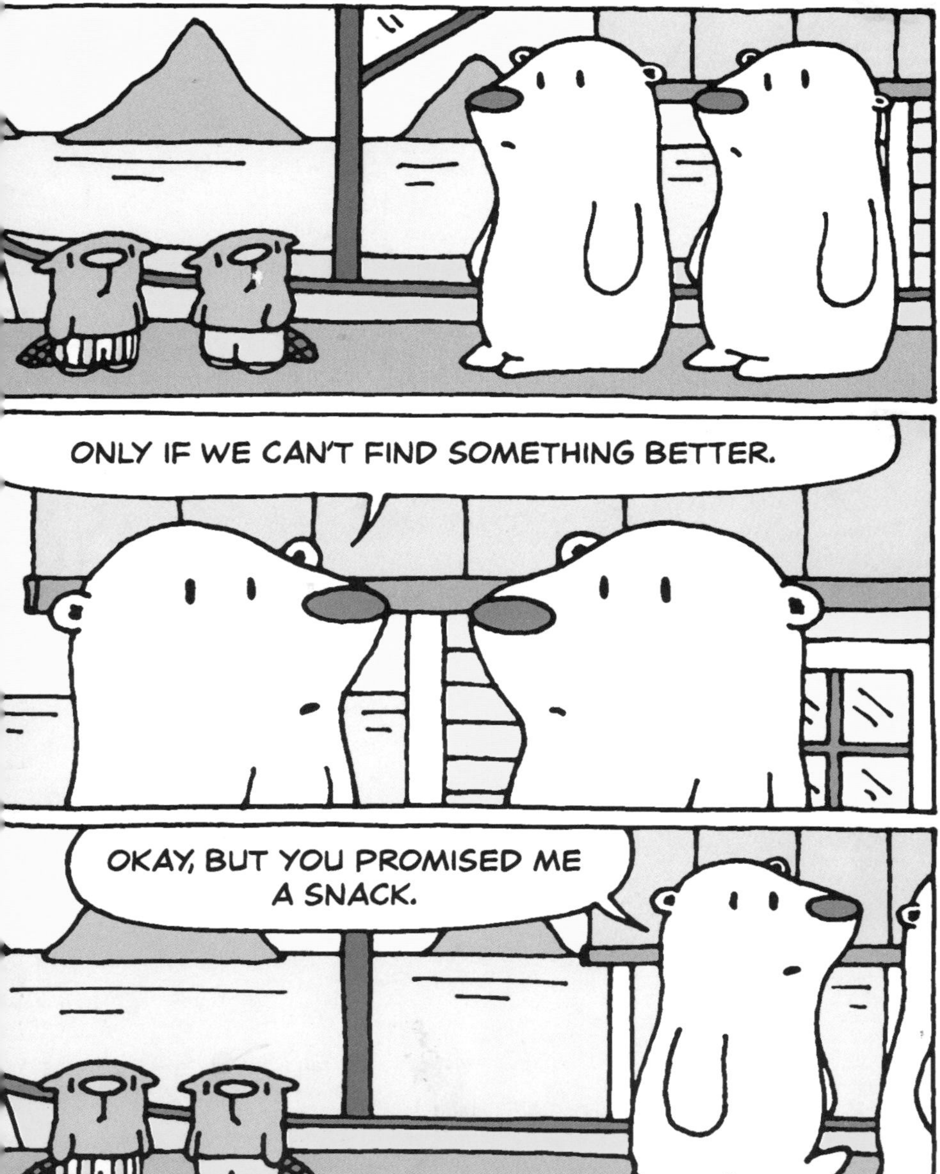
ONLY IF WE CAN'T FIND SOMETHING BETTER.
OKAY, BUT YOU PROMISED ME A SNACK.

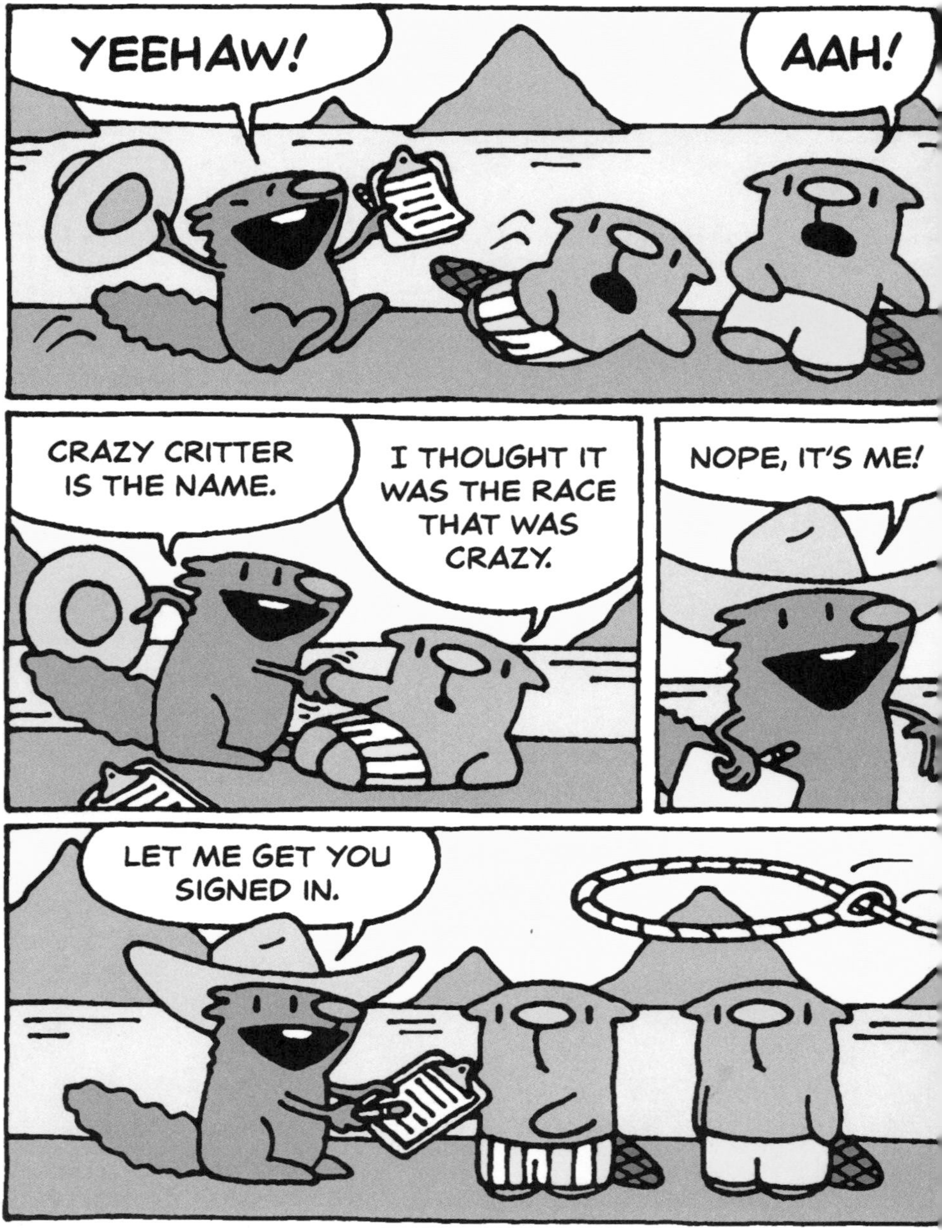
YEEHAW!
AAH!
CRAZY CRITTER IS THE NAME.
I THOUGHT IT WAS THE RACE THAT WAS CRAZY.
NOPE, IT'S ME!
LET ME GET YOU SIGNED IN.

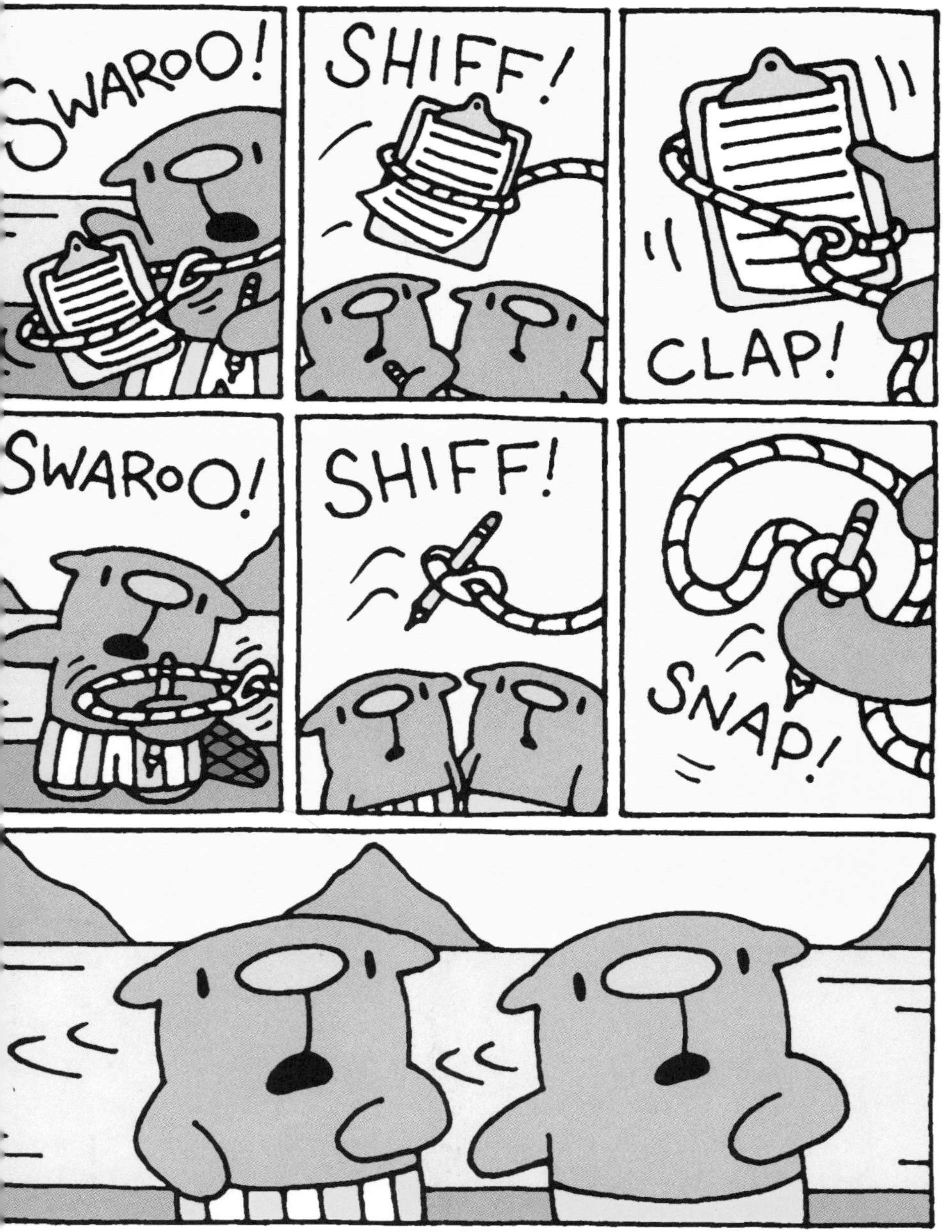
SWAROO!
SHIFF!
CLAP!
SWAROO!
SHIFF!
SNAP!

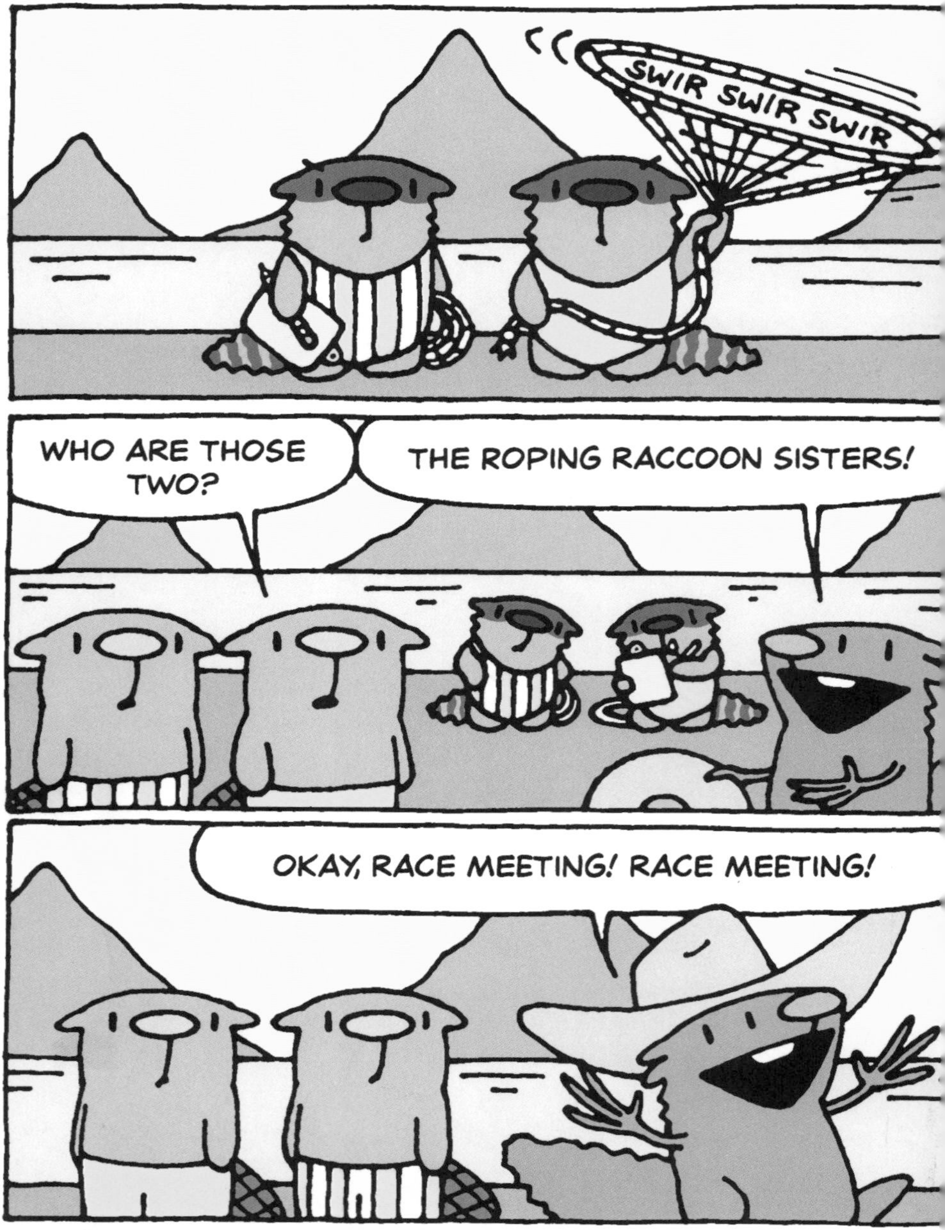
SWIR SWIR SWIR
WHO ARE THOSE TWO?
THE ROPING RACCOON SISTERS!
OKAY, RACE MEETING! RACE MEETING!

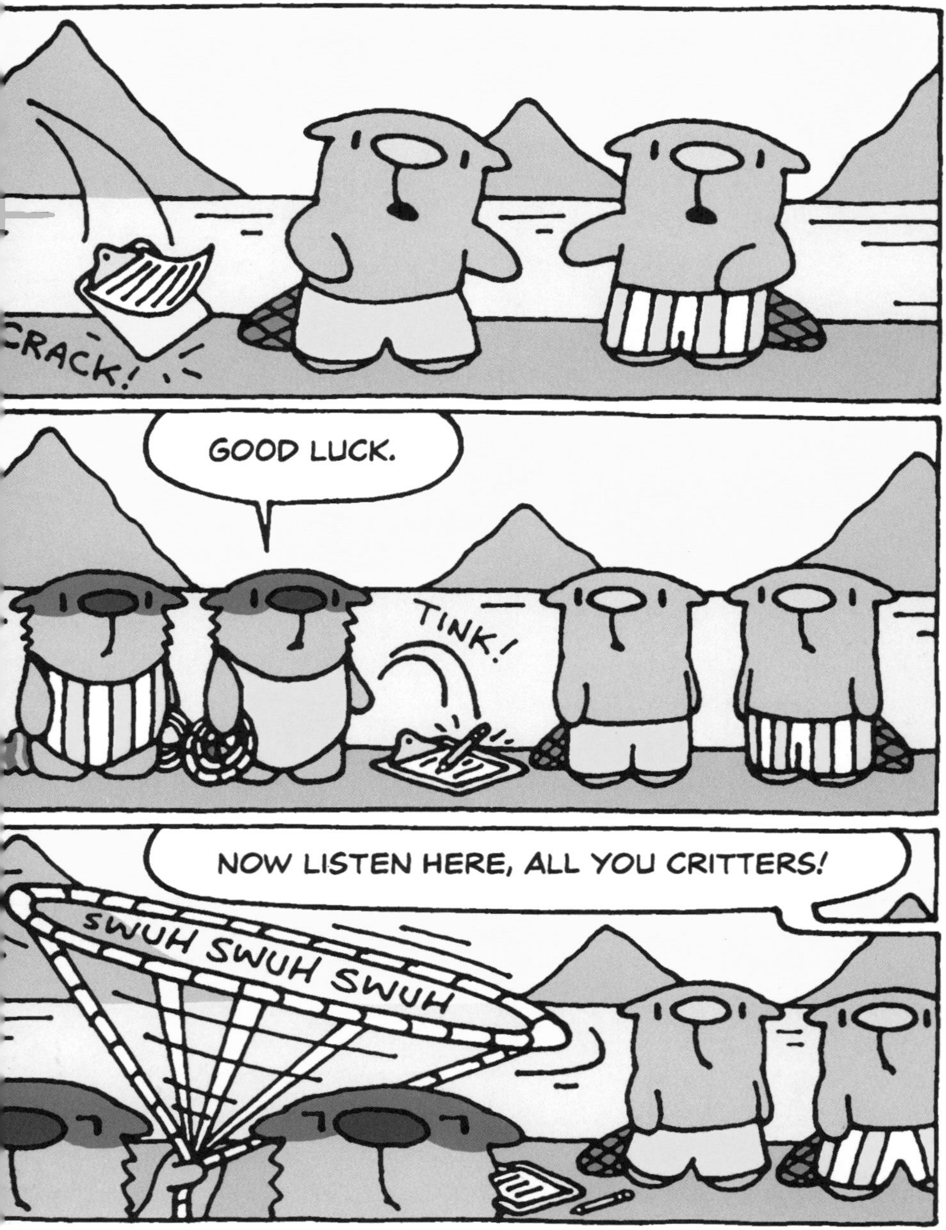
CRACK!
GOOD LUCK.
TINK!
NOW LISTEN HERE, ALL YOU CRITTERS!
SWUH SWUH SWUH

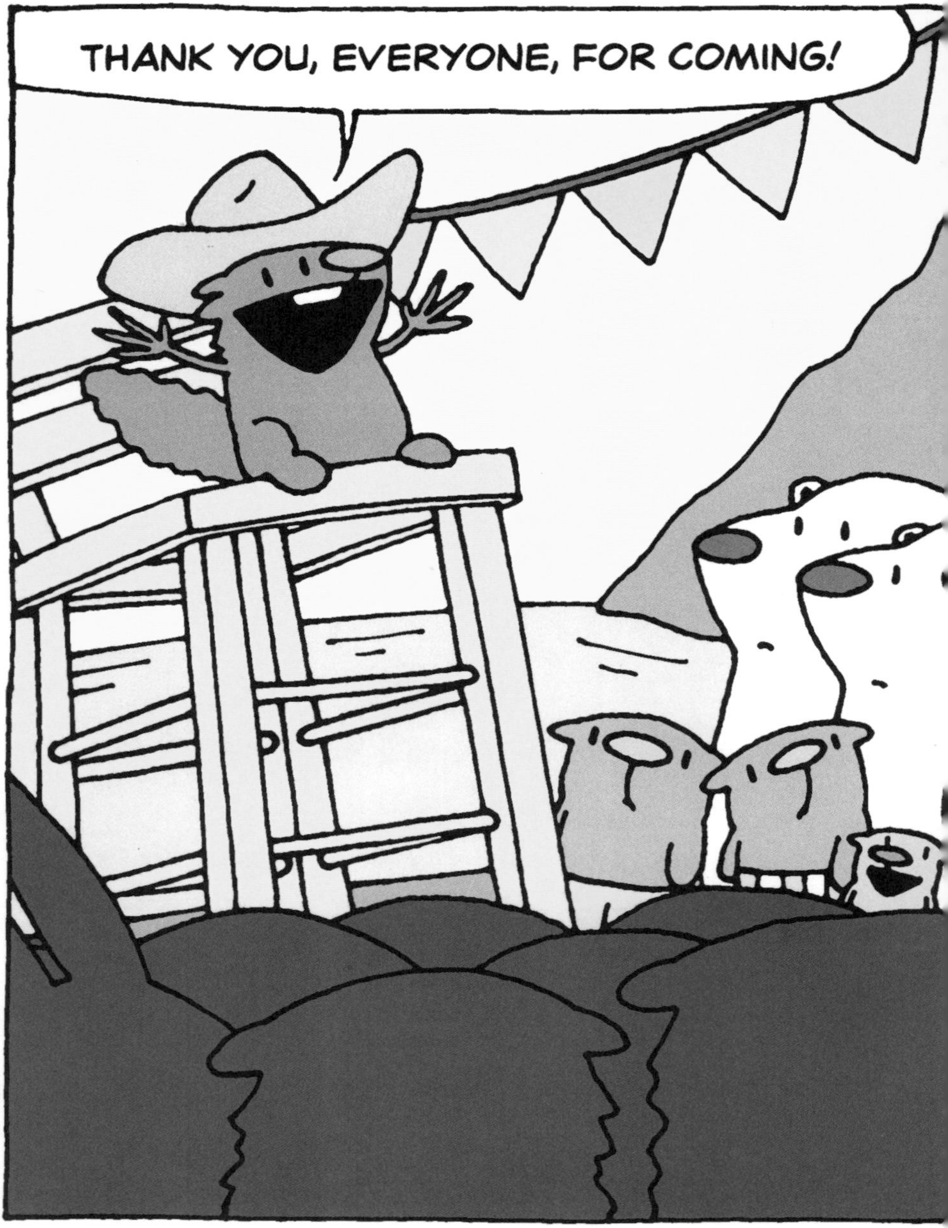
THANK YOU, EVERYONE, FOR COMING!

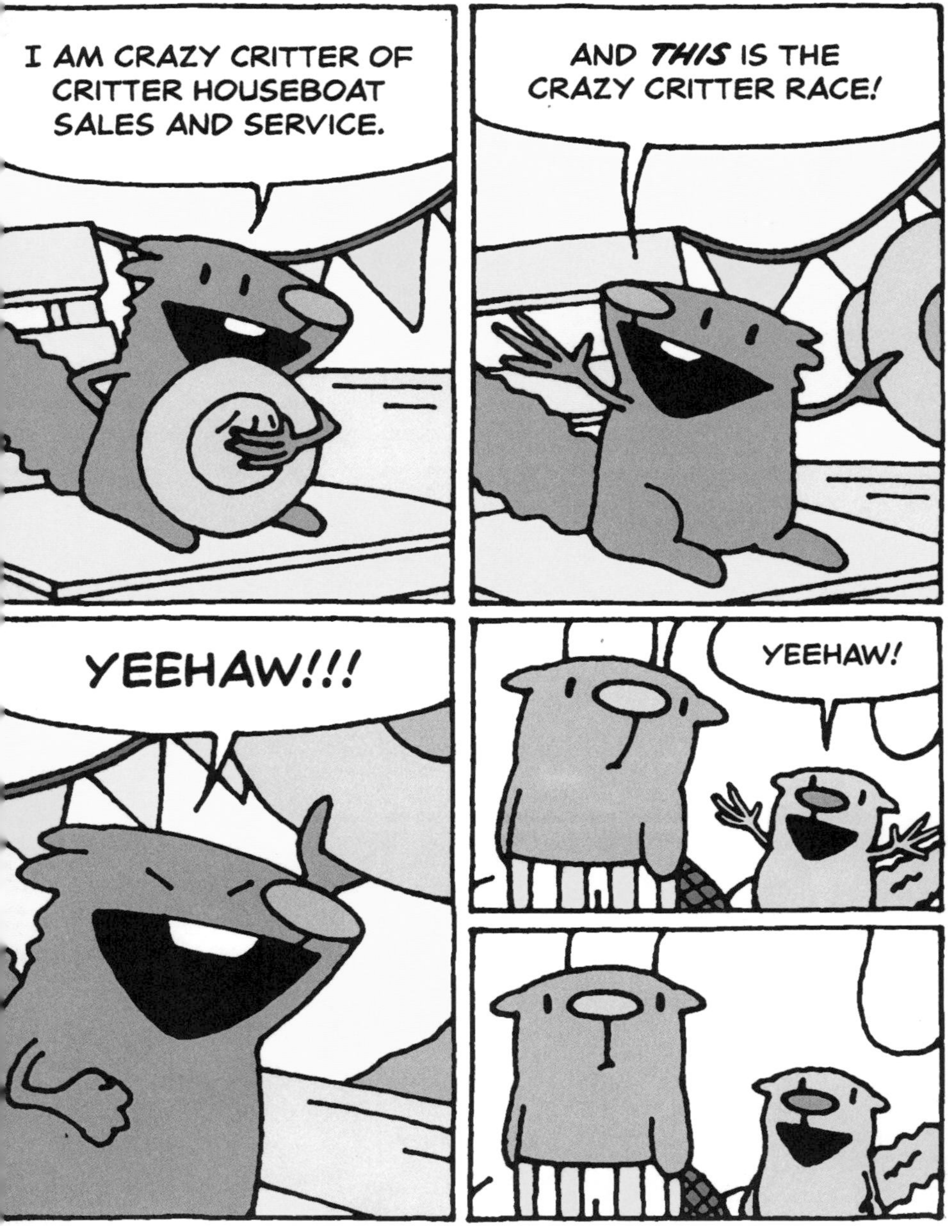
I AM CRAZY CRITTER OF CRITTER HOUSEBOAT SALES AND SERVICE.
AND *THIS* IS THE CRAZY CRITTER RACE!
YEEHAW!!!
YEEHAW!

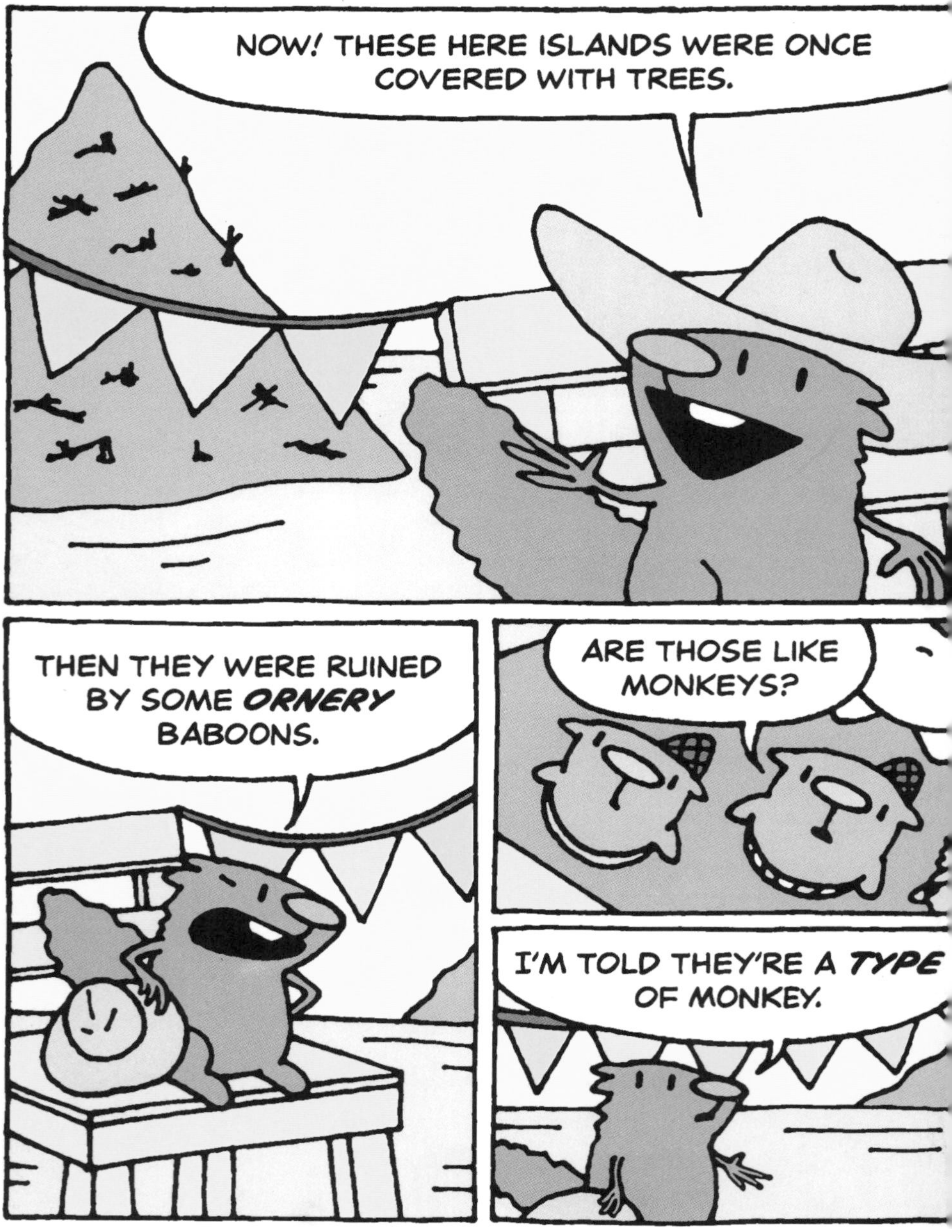
NOW! THESE HERE ISLANDS WERE ONCE COVERED WITH TREES.
THEN THEY WERE RUINED BY SOME *ORNERY* BABOONS.
ARE THOSE LIKE MONKEYS?
I'M TOLD THEY'RE A *TYPE* OF MONKEY.

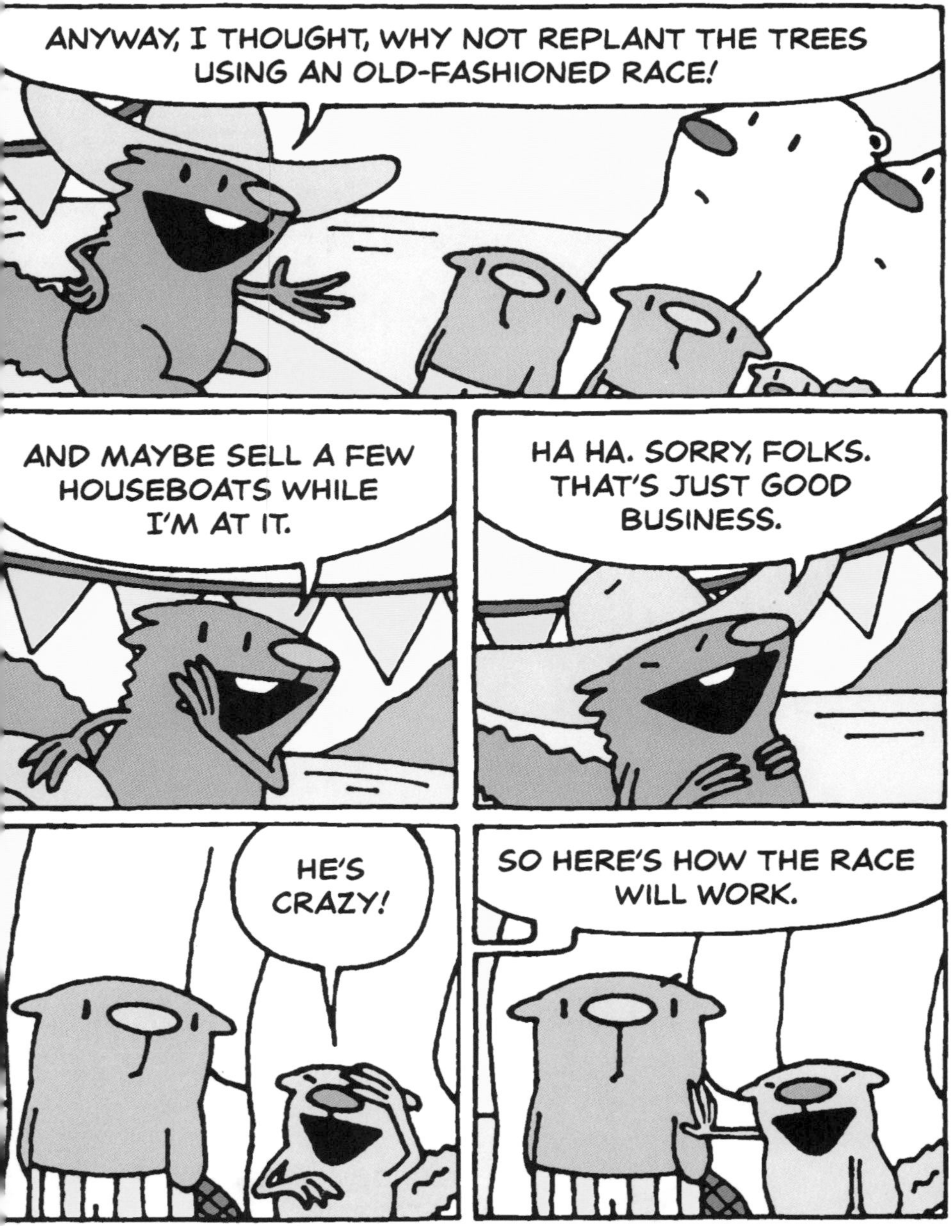

ANYWAY, I THOUGHT, WHY NOT REPLANT THE TREES USING AN OLD-FASHIONED RACE!
AND MAYBE SELL A FEW HOUSEBOATS WHILE I'M AT IT.
HA HA. SORRY, FOLKS. THAT'S JUST GOOD BUSINESS.
HE'S CRAZY!
SO HERE'S HOW THE RACE WILL WORK.

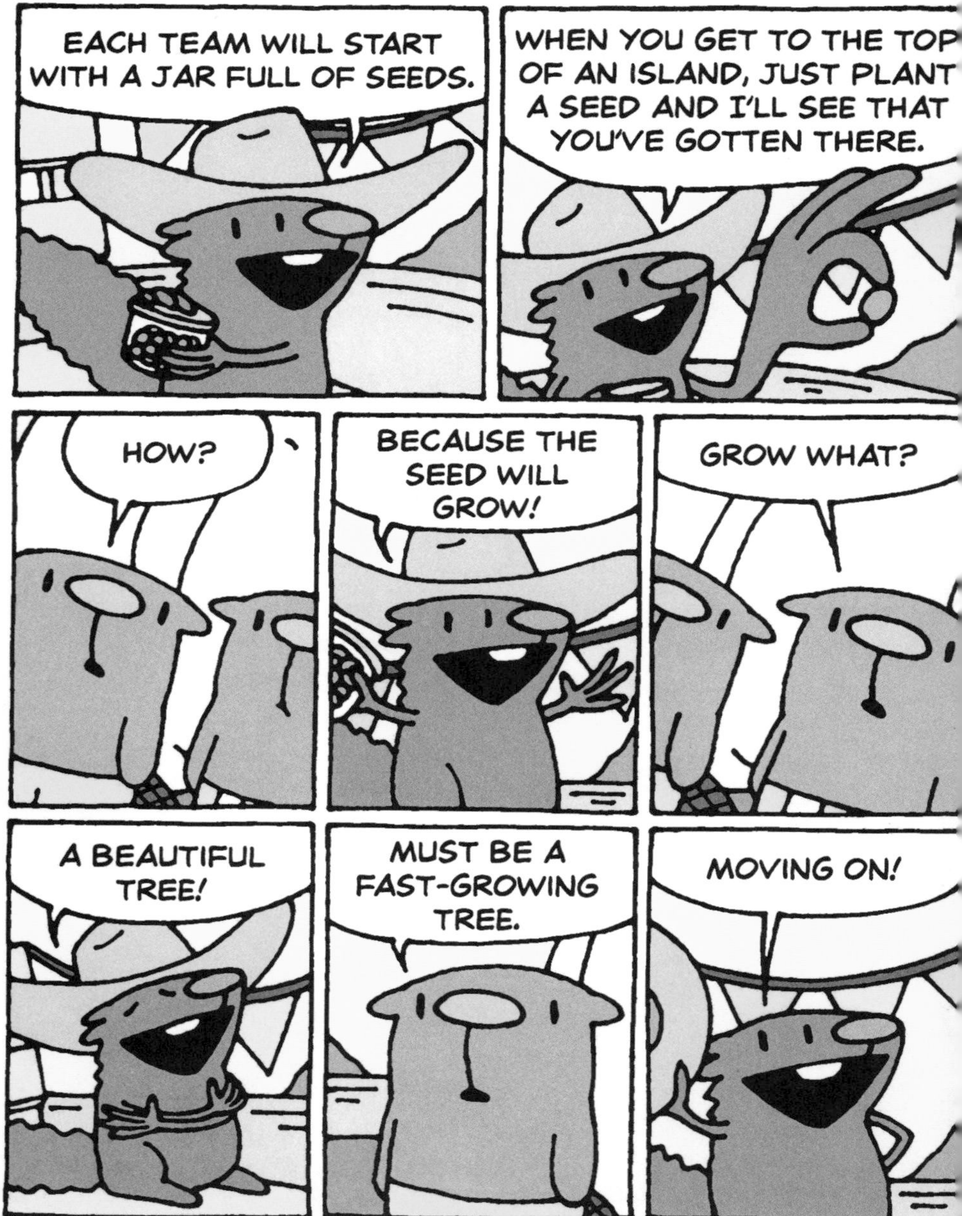
EACH TEAM WILL START WITH A JAR FULL OF SEEDS.
WHEN YOU GET TO THE TOP OF AN ISLAND, JUST PLANT A SEED AND I'LL SEE THAT YOU'VE GOTTEN THERE.
HOW?
BECAUSE THE SEED WILL GROW!
GROW WHAT?
A BEAUTIFUL TREE!
MUST BE A FAST-GROWING TREE.
MOVING ON!

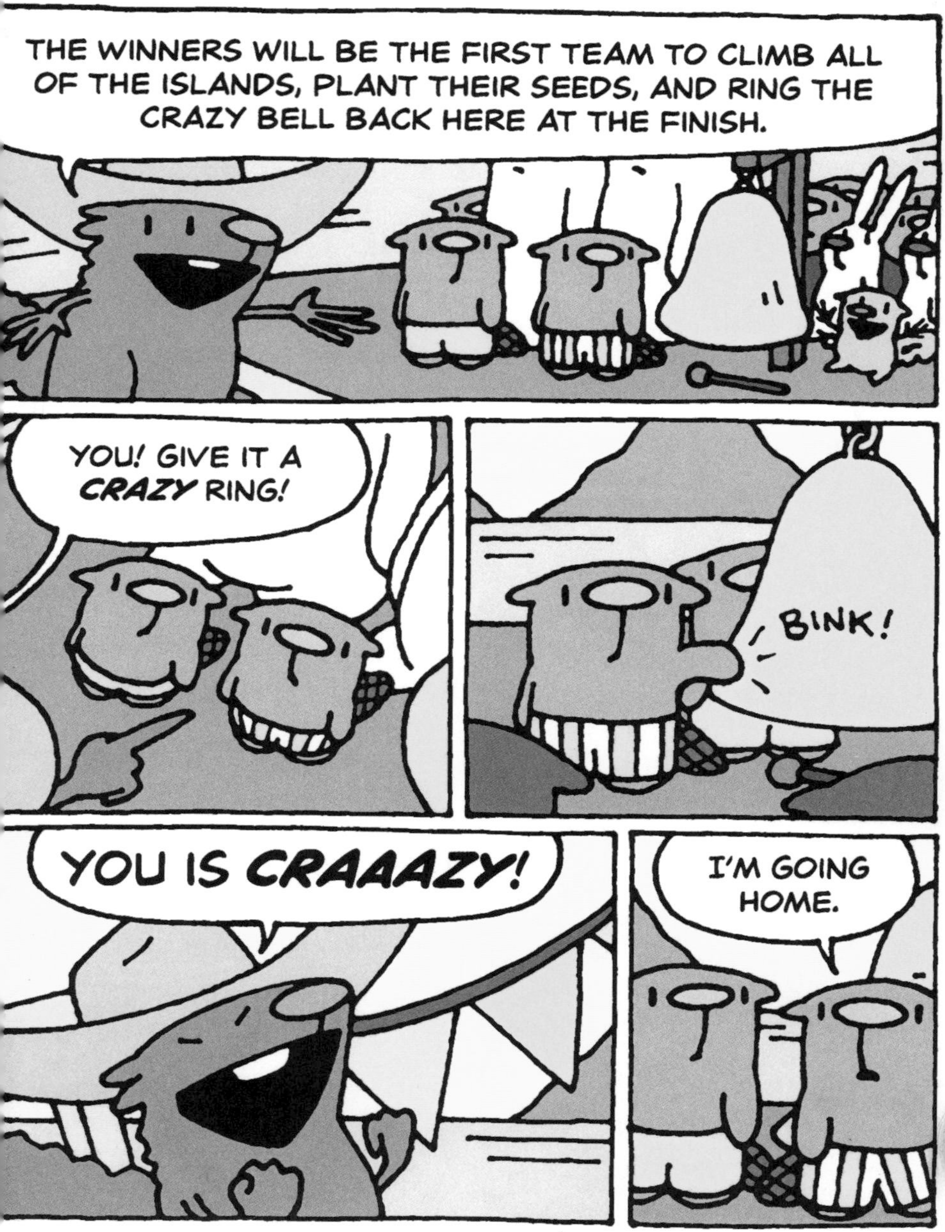
THE WINNERS WILL BE THE FIRST TEAM TO CLIMB ALL OF THE ISLANDS, PLANT THEIR SEEDS, AND RING THE CRAZY BELL BACK HERE AT THE FINISH.
YOU! GIVE IT A *CRAZY* RING!
BINK!
YOU IS *CRAAAZY!*
I'M GOING HOME.

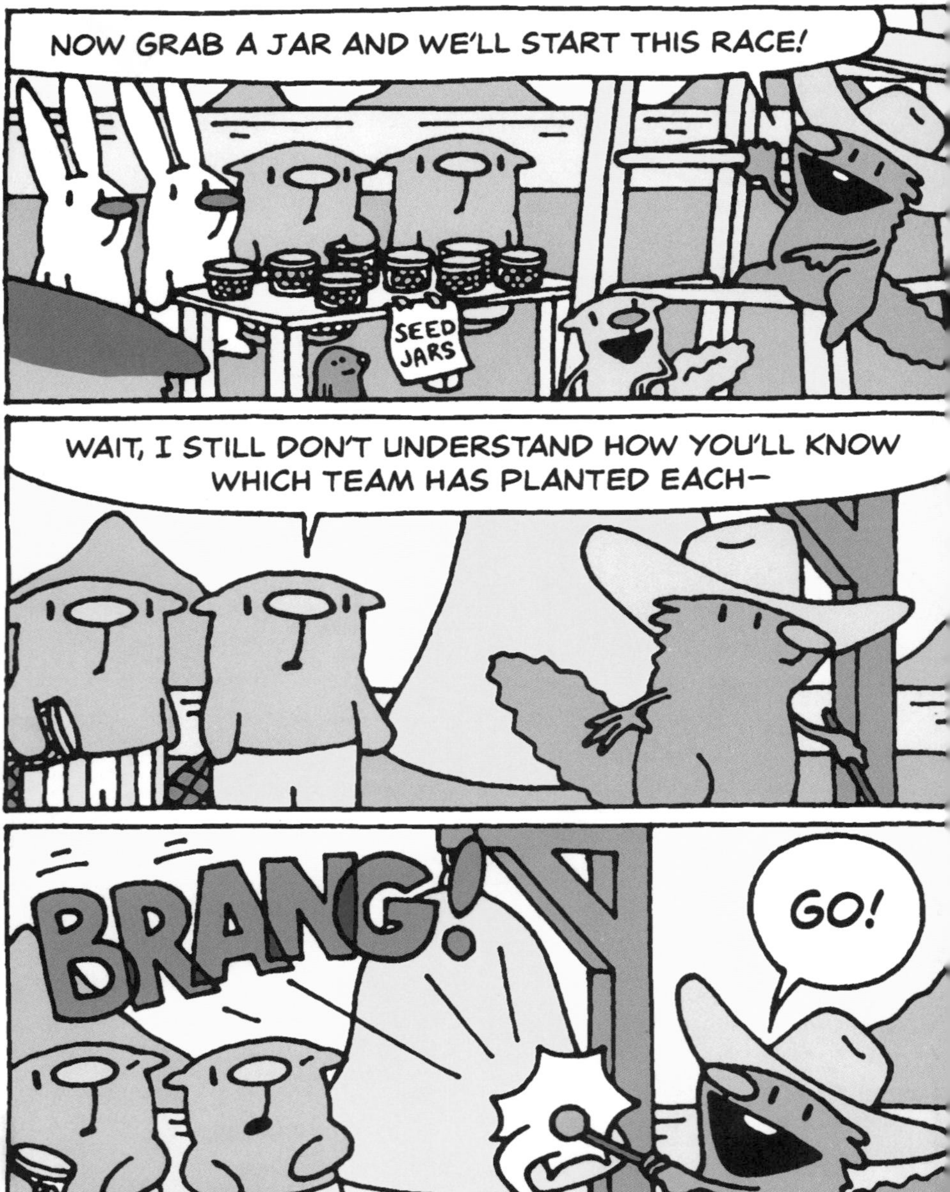
NOW GRAB A JAR AND WE'LL START THIS RACE!
SEED JARS
WAIT, I STILL DON'T UNDERSTAND HOW YOU'LL KNOW WHICH TEAM HAS PLANTED EACH—
BRANG!
GO!

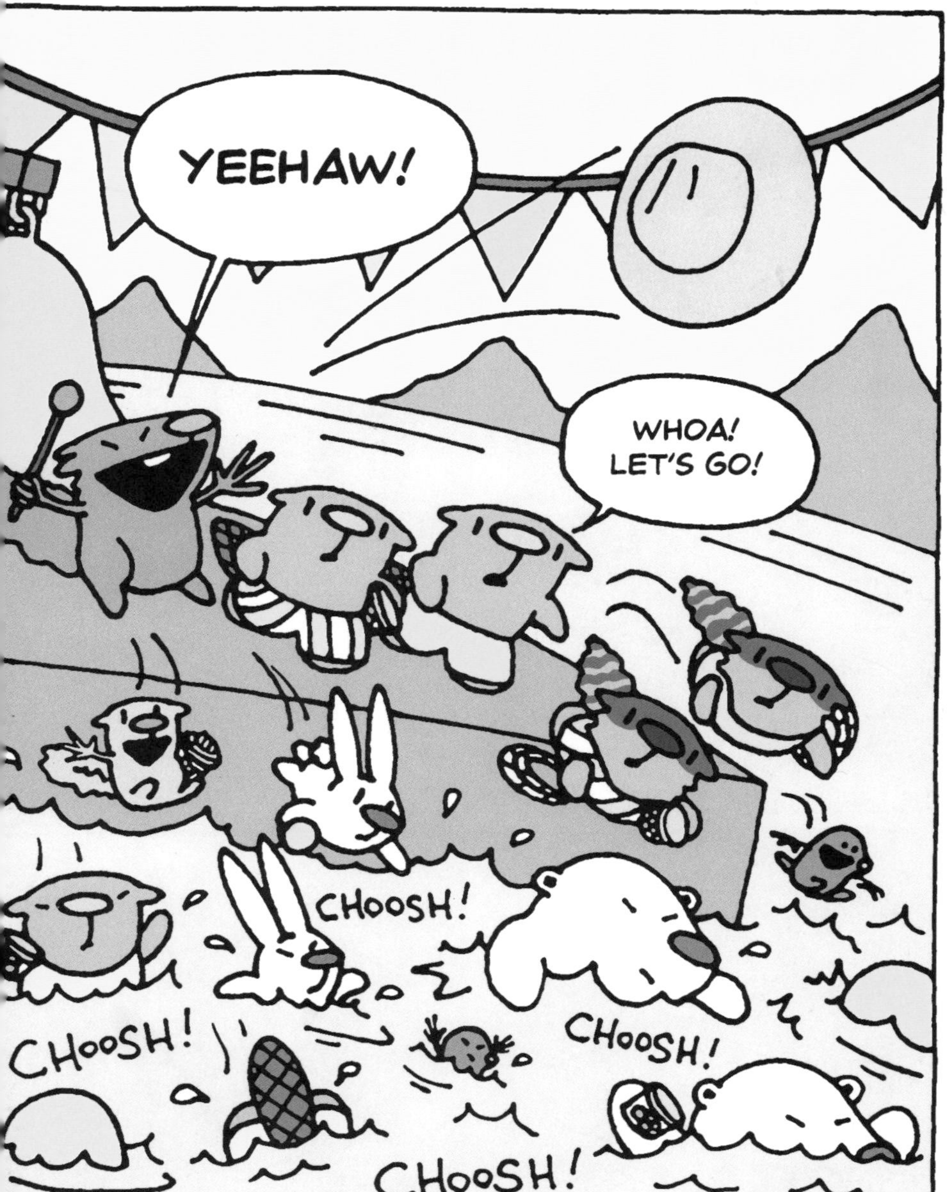
YEEHAW!
WHOA! LET'S GO!
CHOOSH!
CHOOSH!
CHOOSH!
CHOOSH!

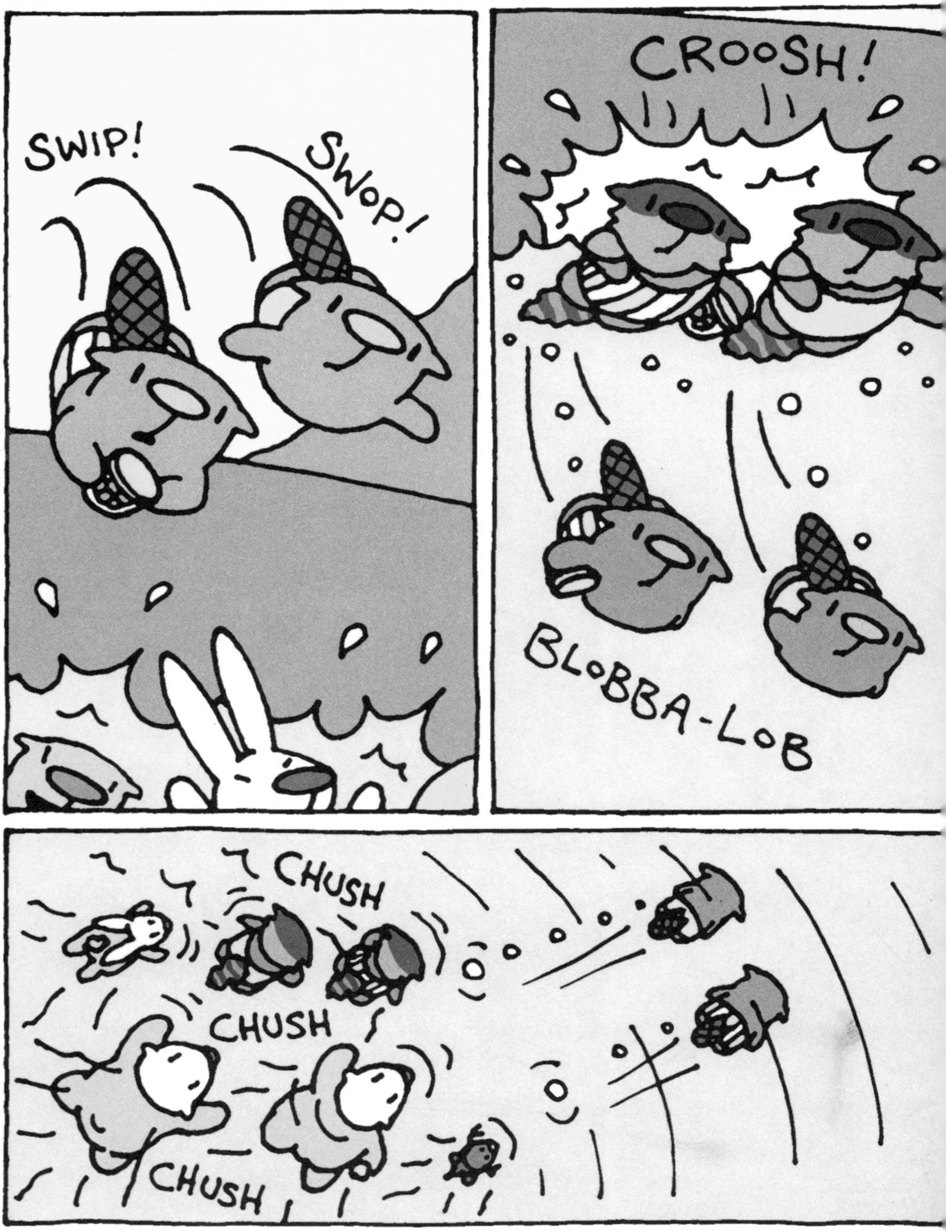
SWIP!
SWOP!
CROOSH!
BLOBBA-LOB
CHUSH
CHUSH
CHUSH

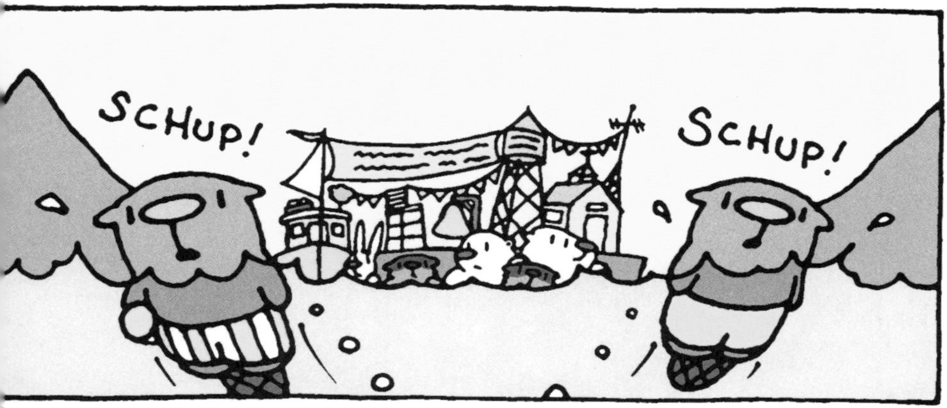
SCHUP!
SCHUP!

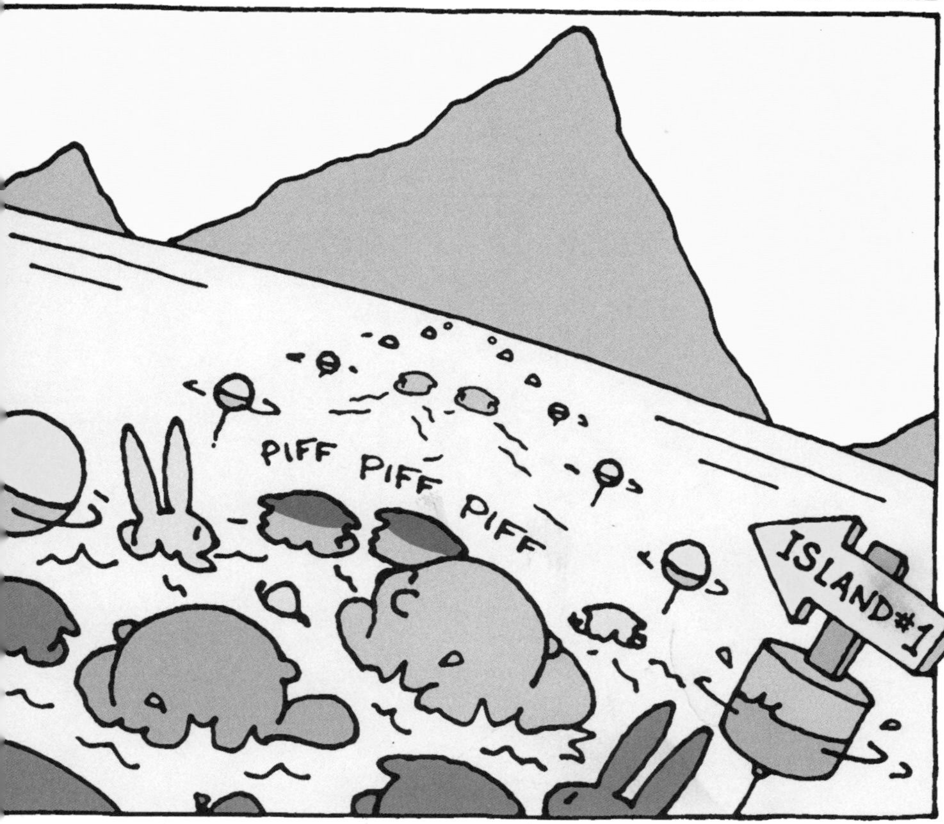
PIFF PIFF PIFF
ISLAND #1

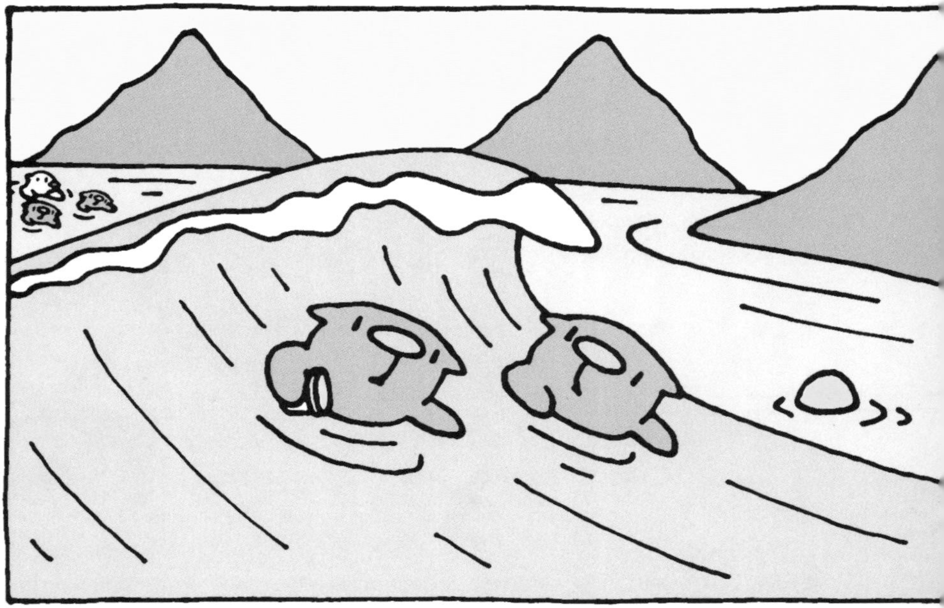

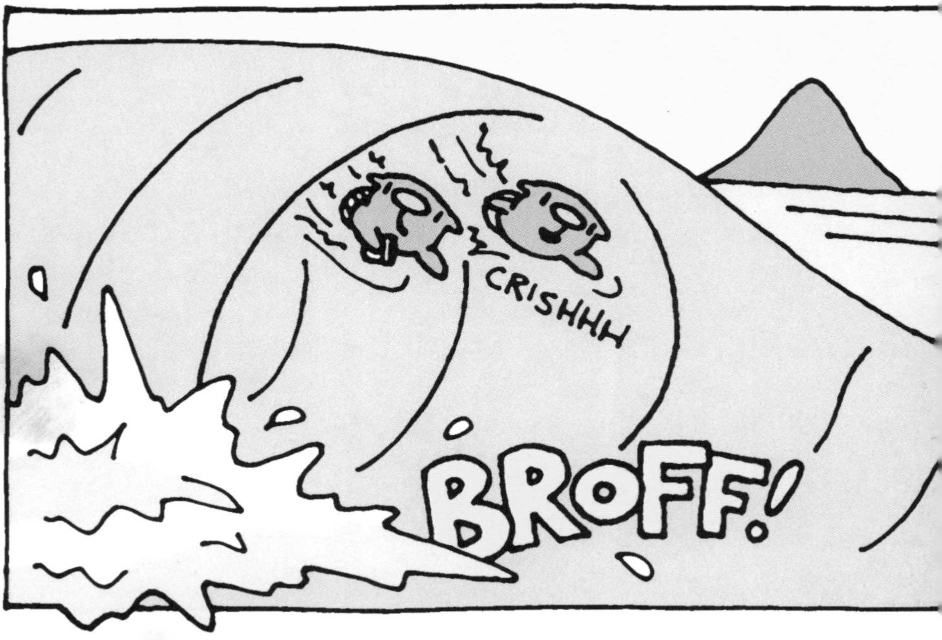
CRISHHH
BROFF!

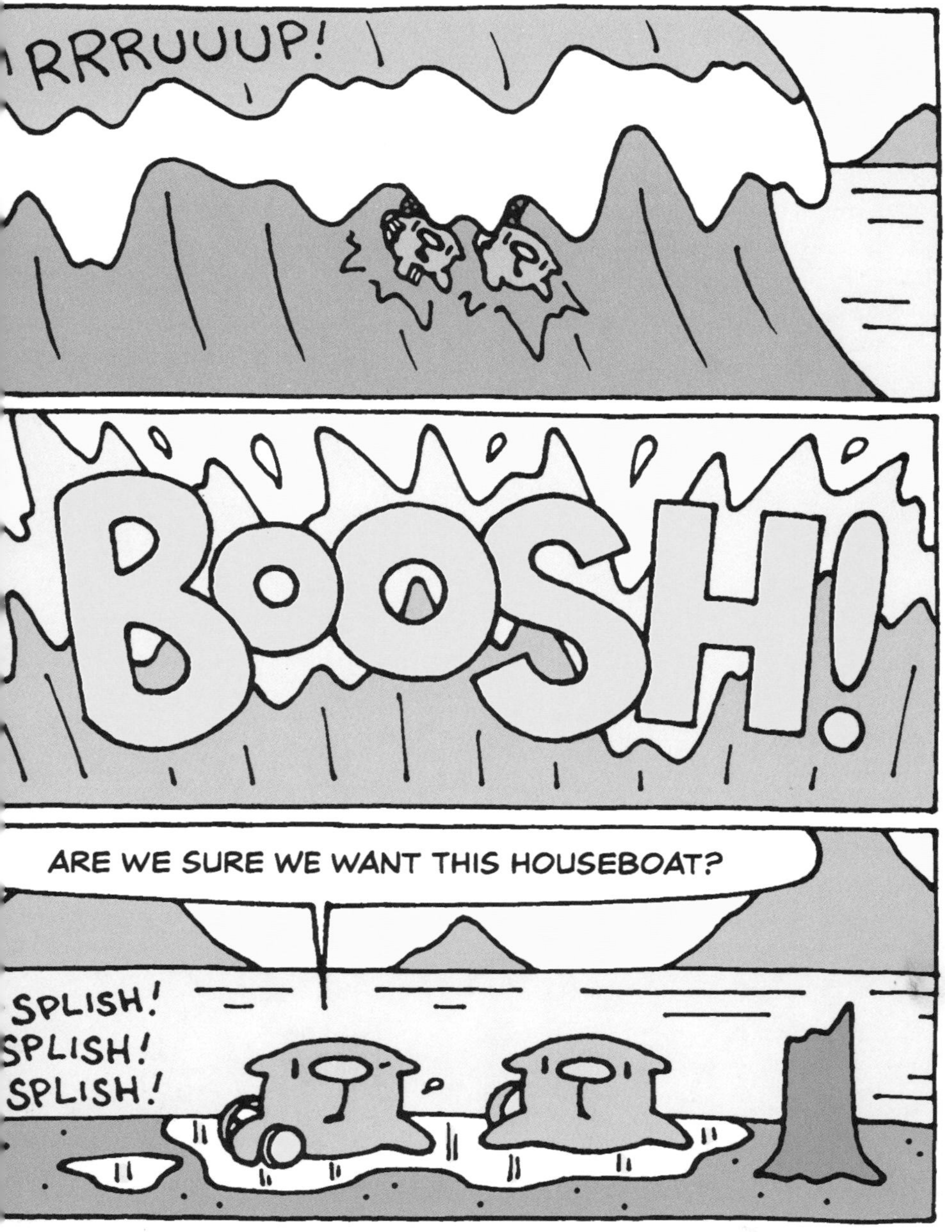
RRRUUUP!
BOOSH!
ARE WE SURE WE WANT THIS HOUSEBOAT?
SPLISH!
SPLISH!
SPLISH!

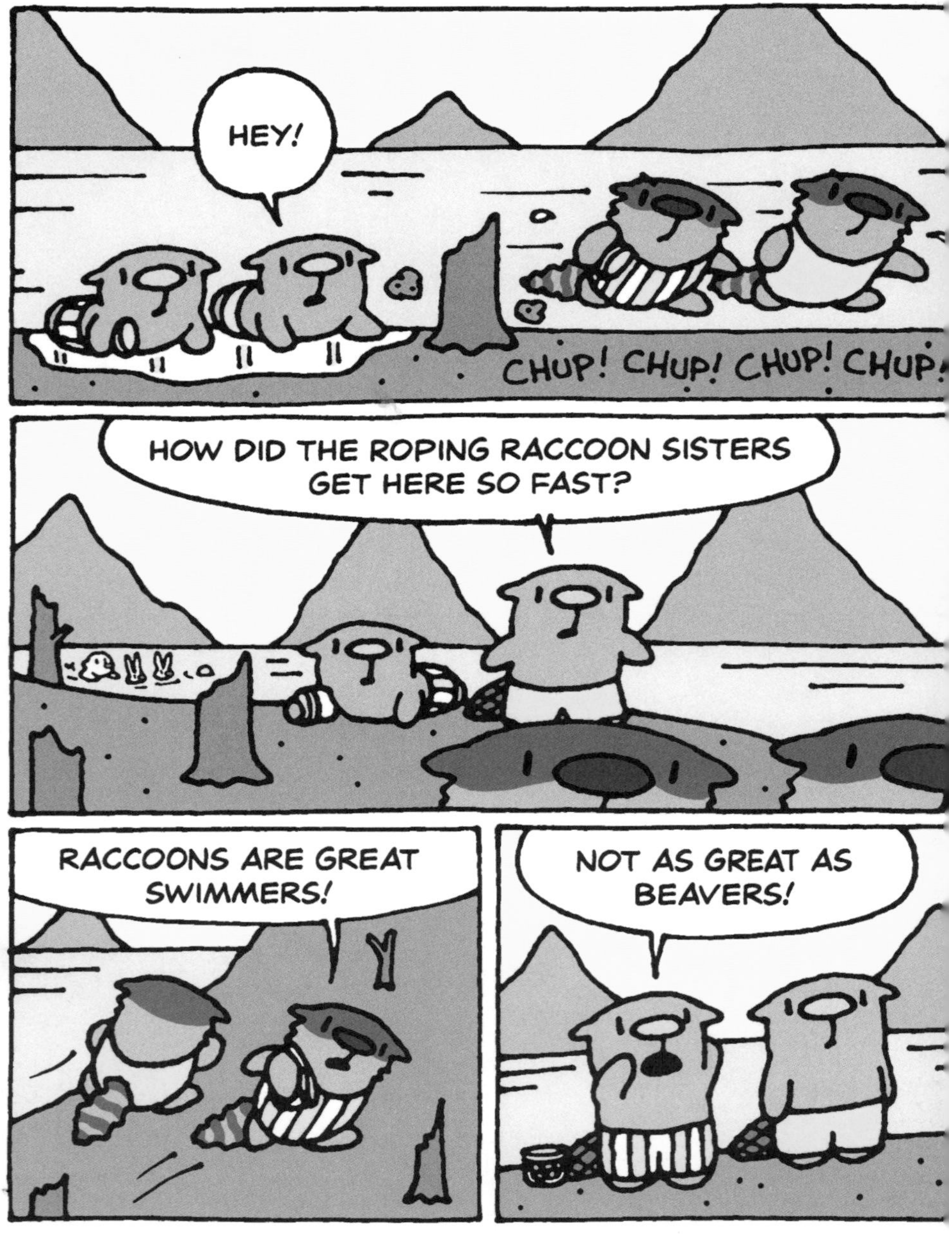
HEY!
CHUP! CHUP! CHUP! CHUP!
HOW DID THE ROPING RACCOON SISTERS GET HERE SO FAST?
RACCOONS ARE GREAT SWIMMERS!
NOT AS GREAT AS BEAVERS!

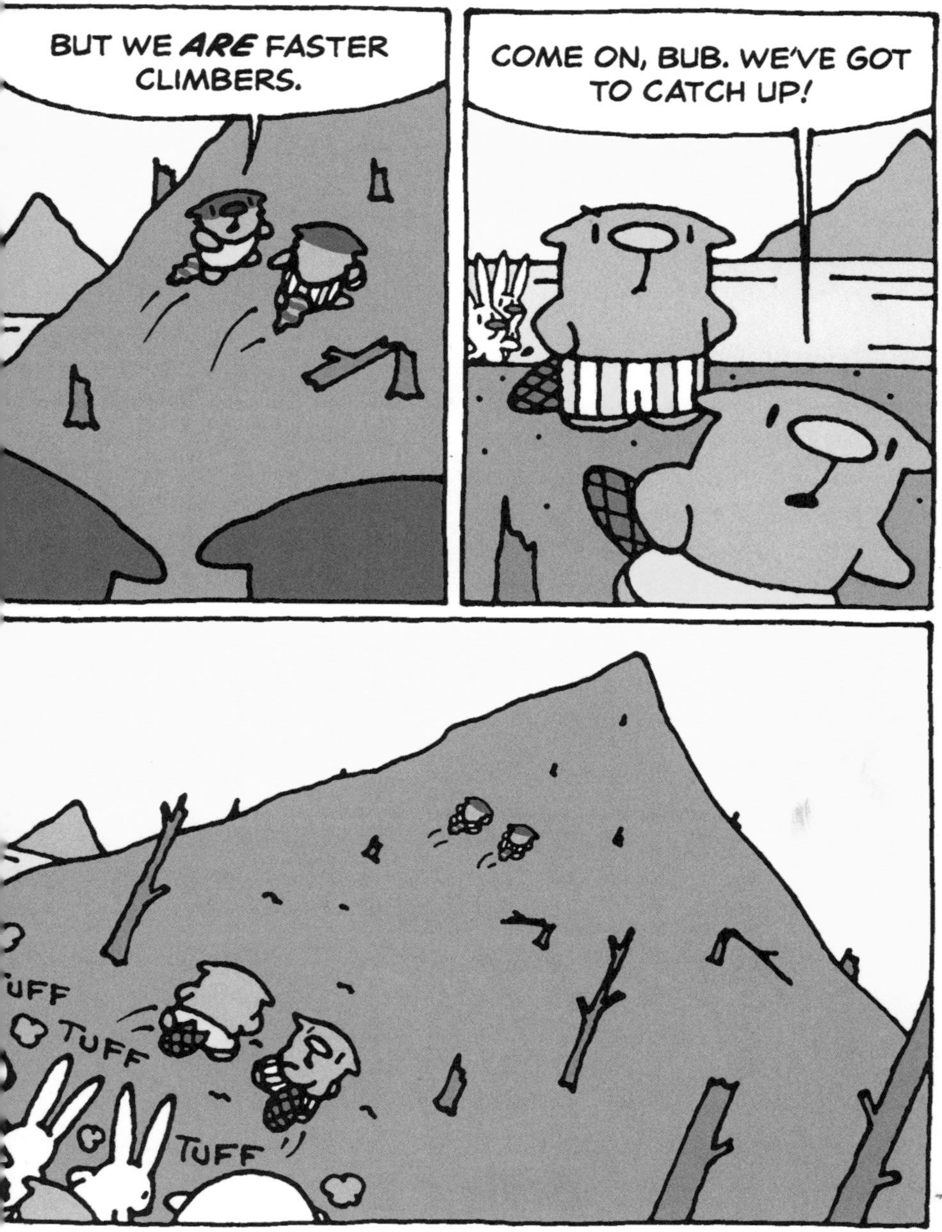
BUT WE ARE FASTER CLIMBERS.
COME ON, BUB. WE'VE GOT TO CATCH UP!
UFF
TUFF
TUFF

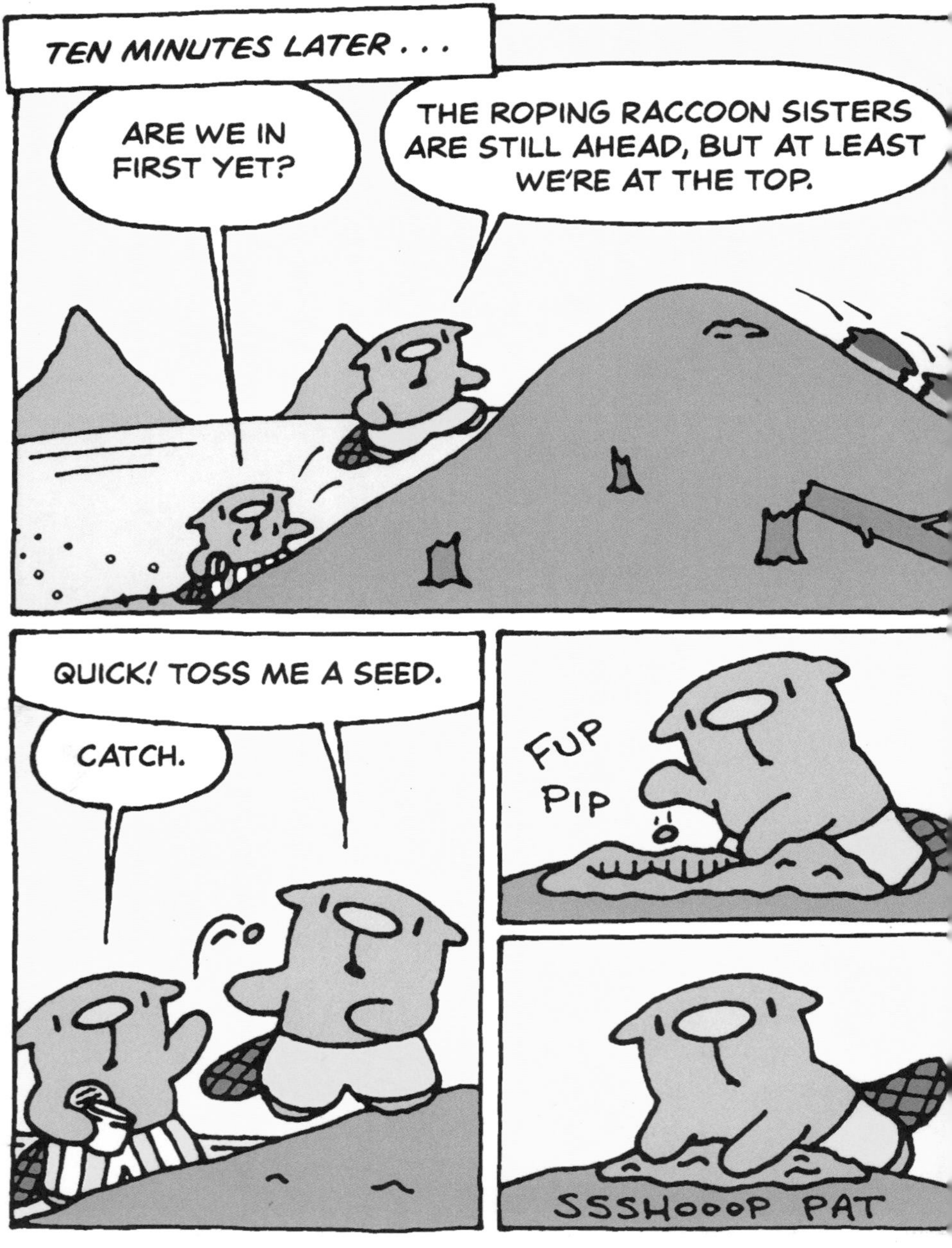

TEN MINUTES LATER . . .
ARE WE IN FIRST YET?
THE ROPING RACCOON SISTERS ARE STILL AHEAD, BUT AT LEAST WE'RE AT THE TOP.
QUICK! TOSS ME A SEED.
CATCH.
FUP
PIP
SSSHOOOP PAT

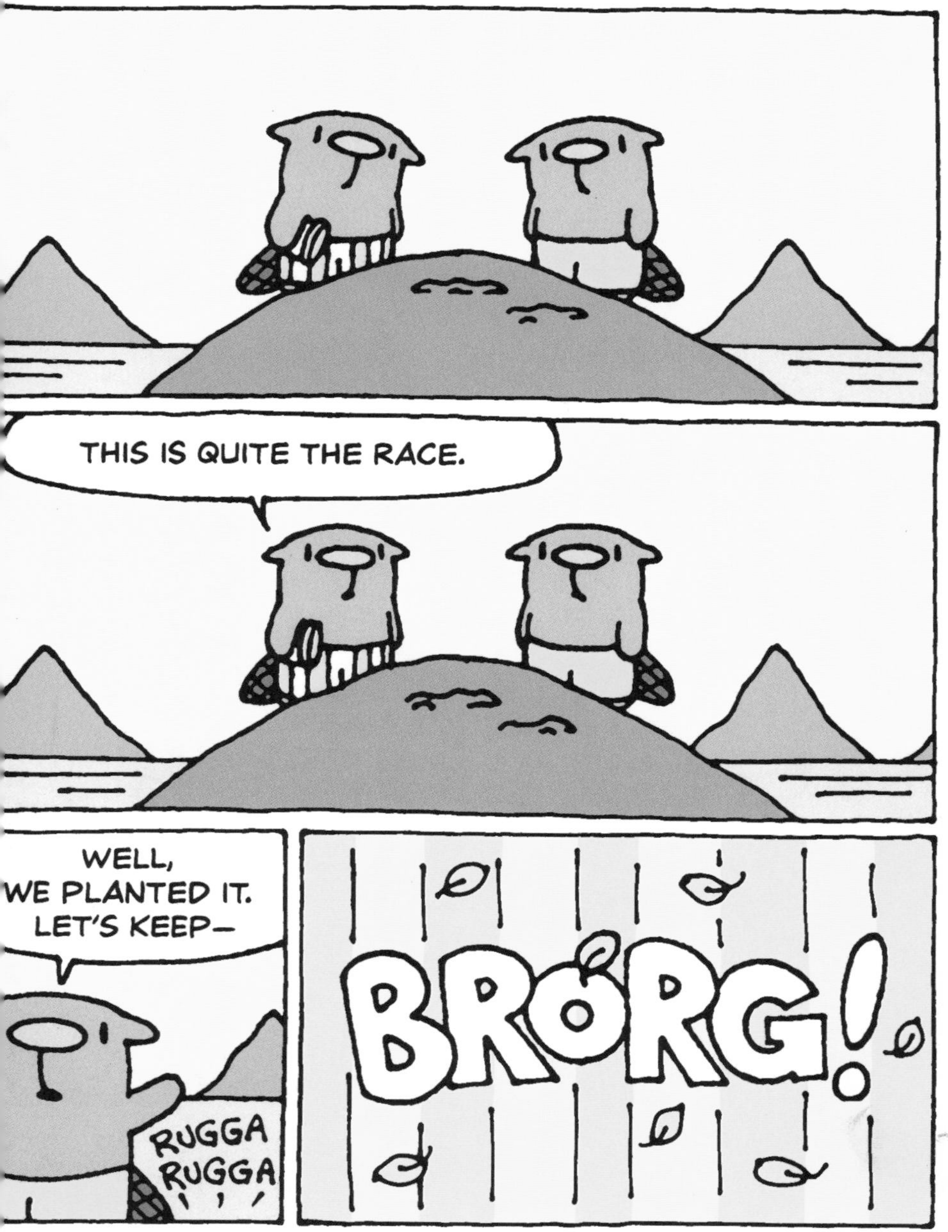
THIS IS QUITE THE RACE.
WELL, WE PLANTED IT. LET'S KEEP—
RUGGA RUGGA
BRORG!

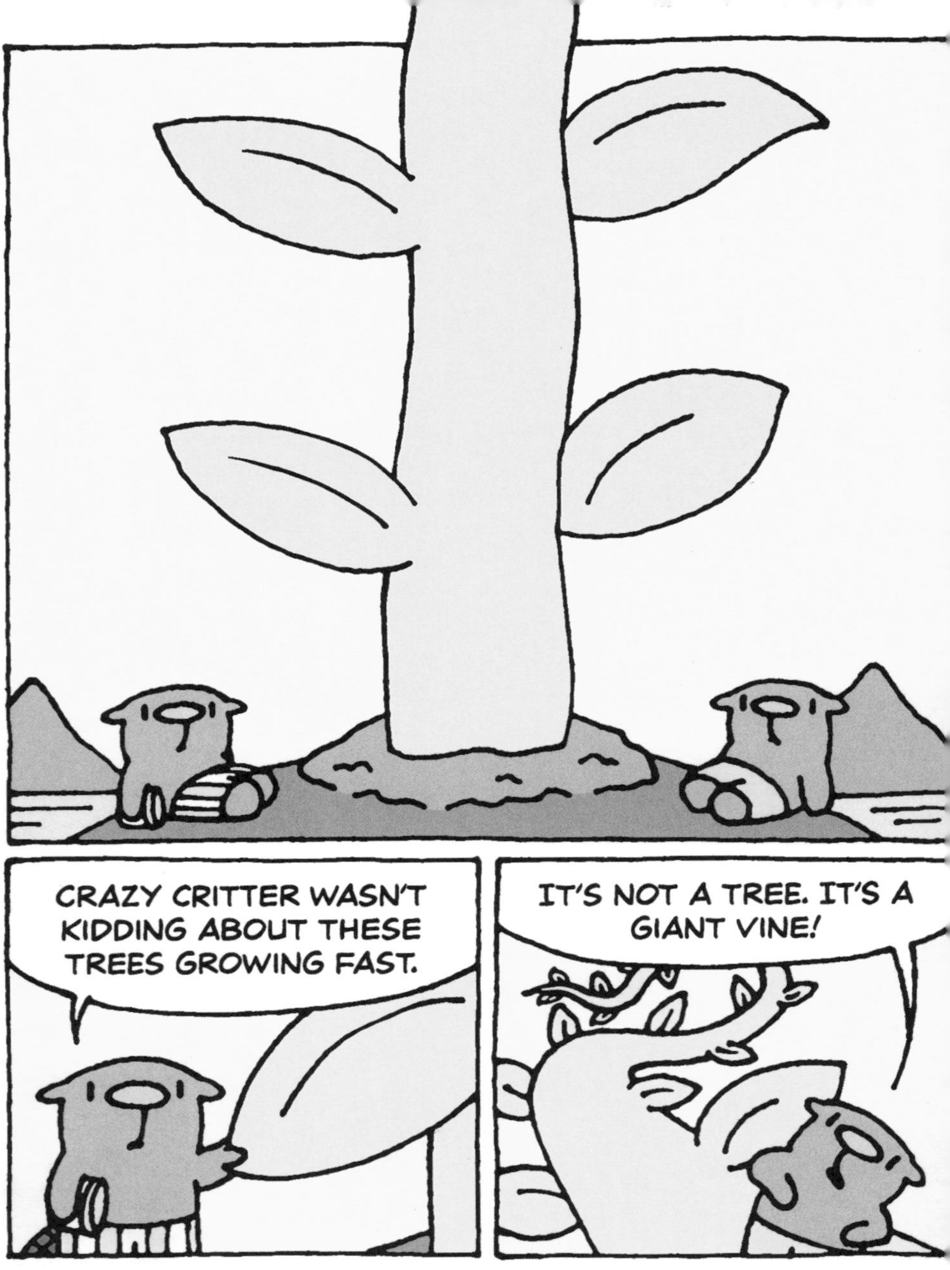
CRAZY CRITTER WASN'T KIDDING ABOUT THESE TREES GROWING FAST.
IT'S NOT A TREE. IT'S A GIANT VINE!

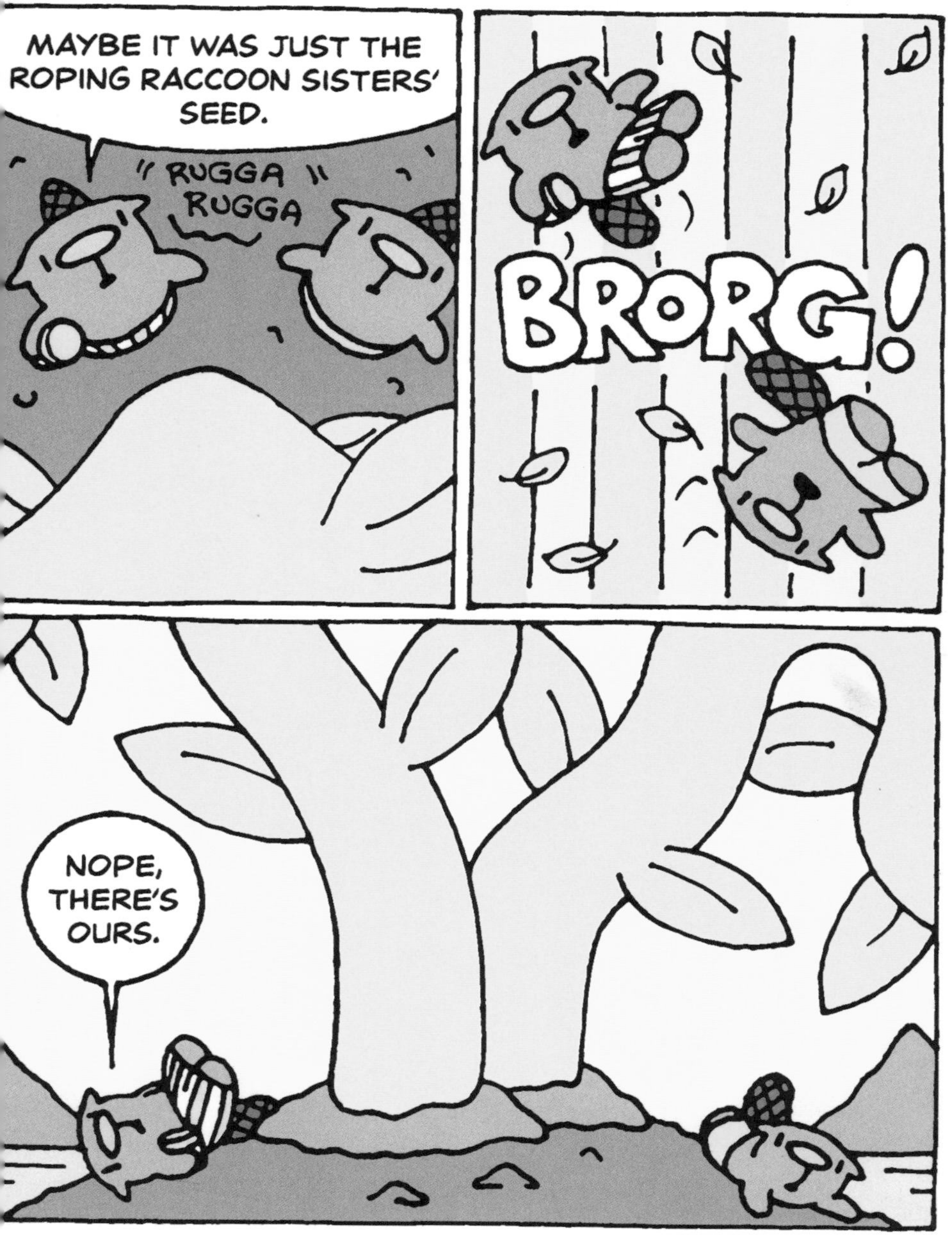
MAYBE IT WAS JUST THE ROPING RACCOON SISTERS' SEED.
" RUGGA RUGGA "
BRORG!
NOPE, THERE'S OURS.

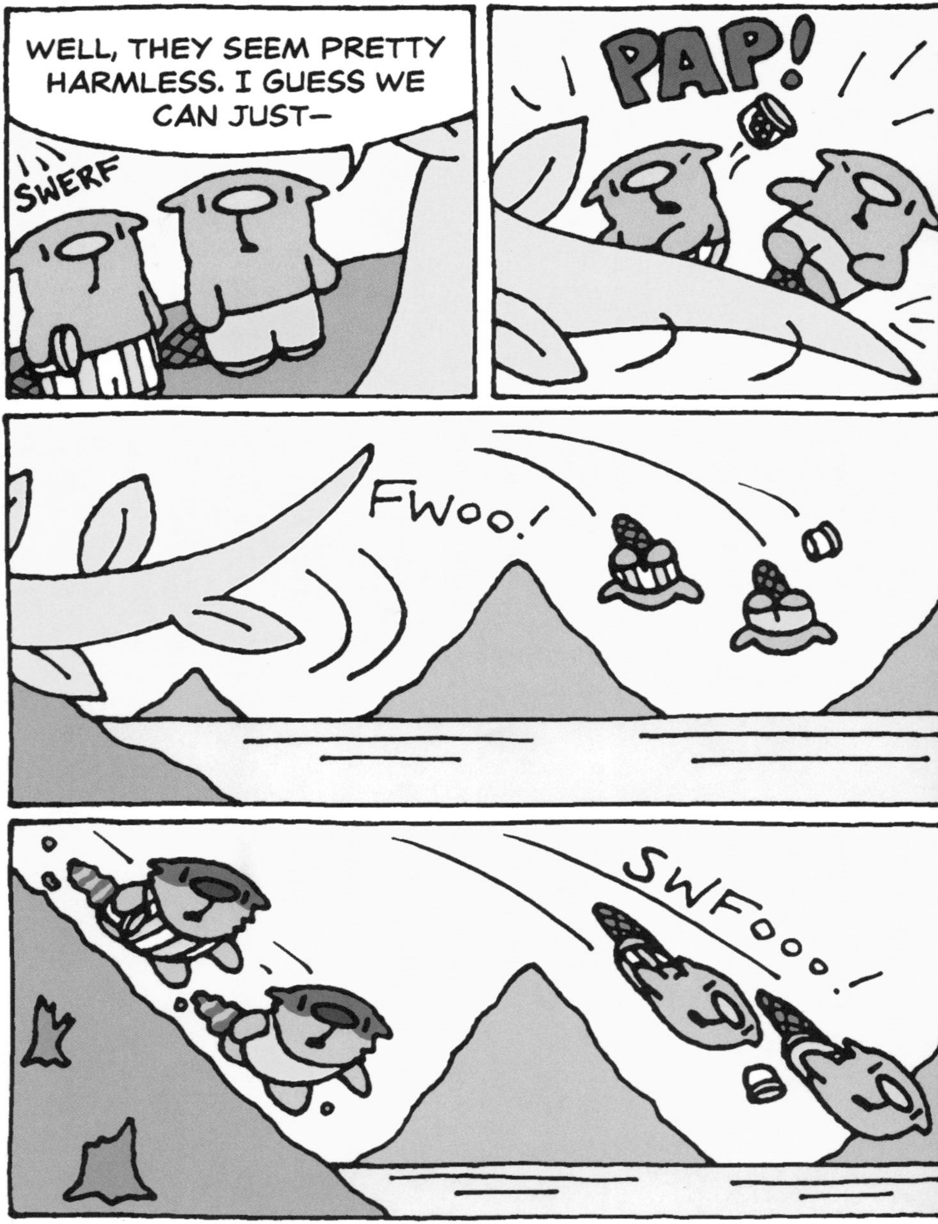
WELL, THEY SEEM PRETTY HARMLESS. I GUESS WE CAN JUST—
SWERF
PAP!
FWOO.!
SWFOOO..!

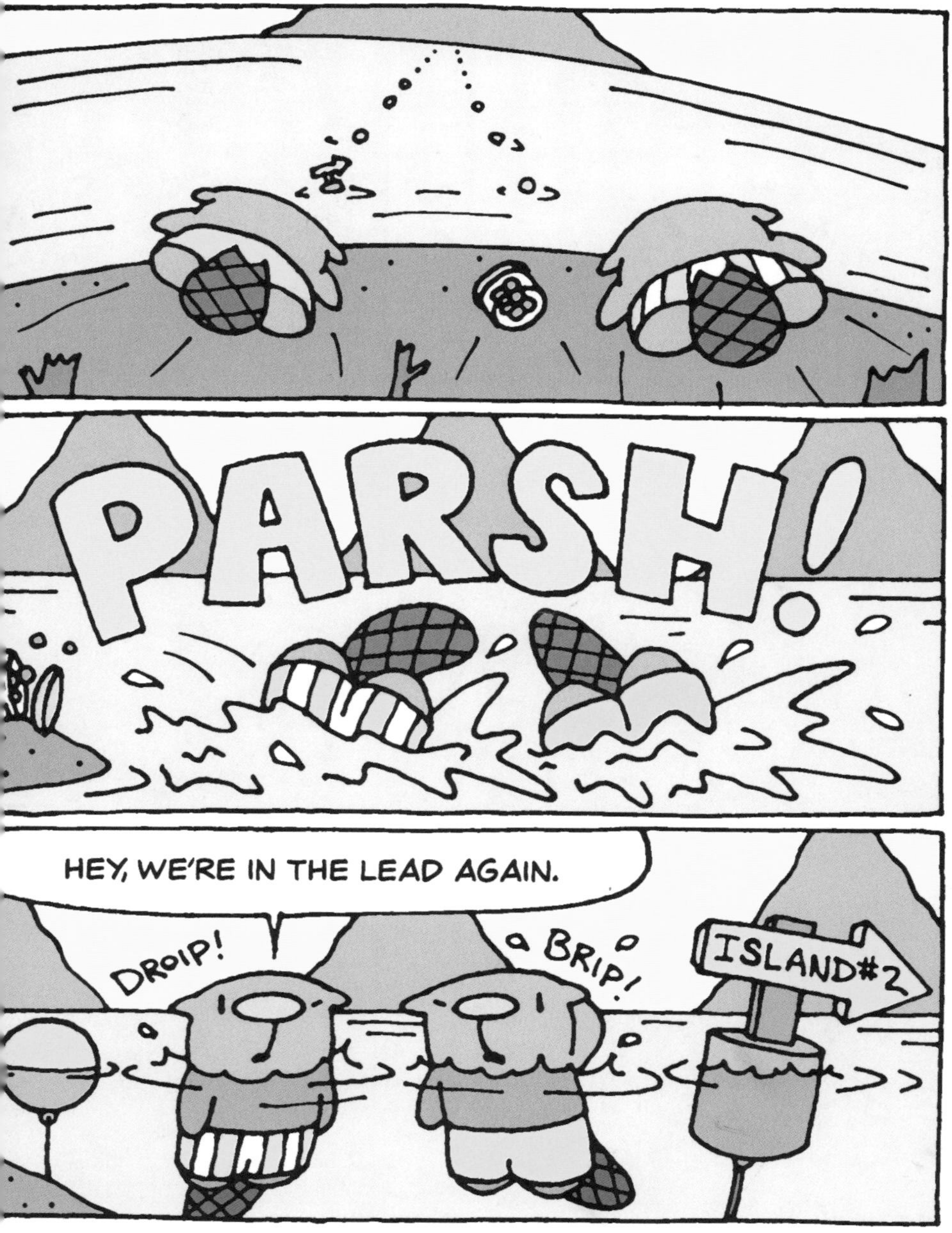
PARSH!
HEY, WE'RE IN THE LEAD AGAIN.
DROIP!
BRIP!
ISLAND#2

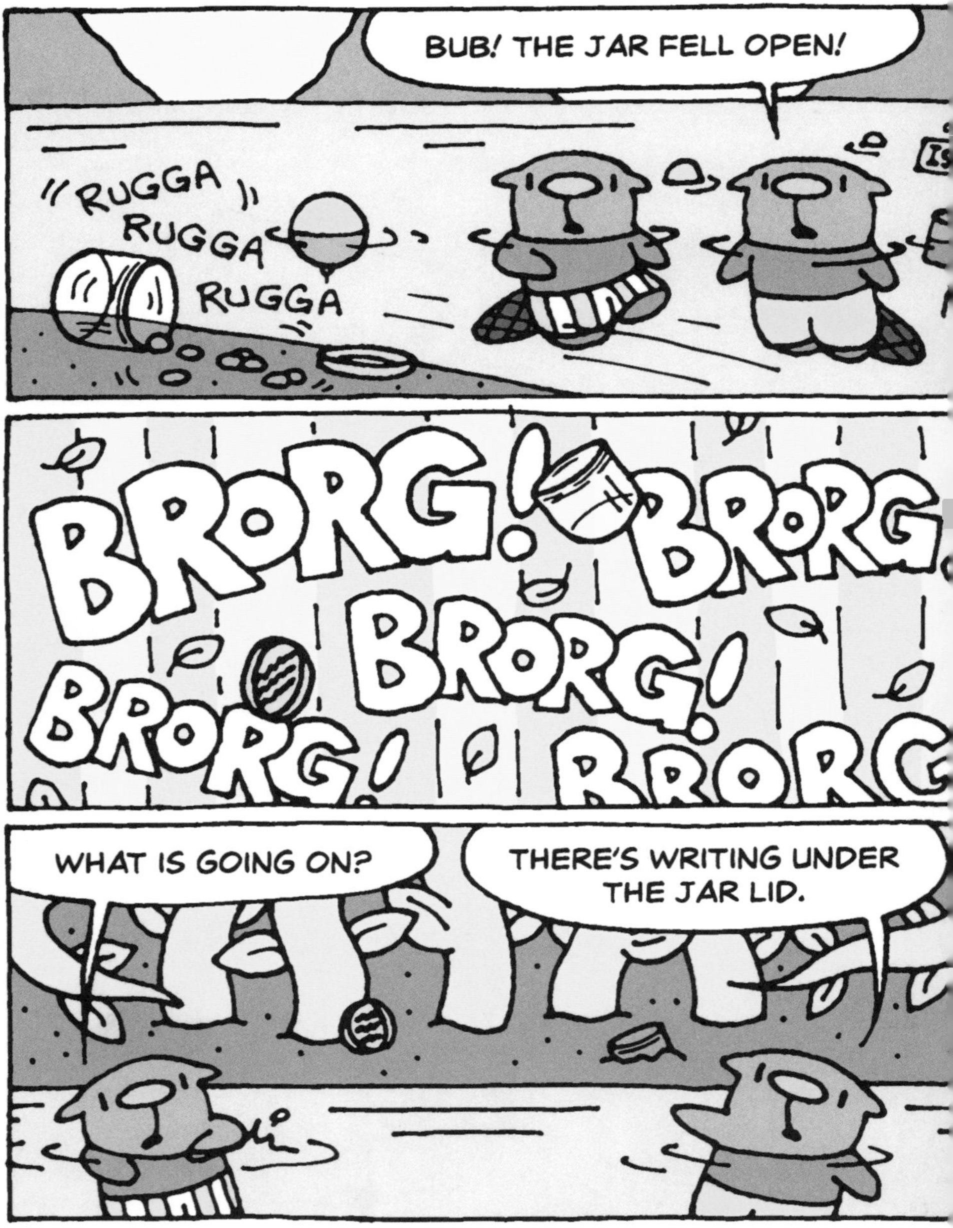
BUB! THE JAR FELL OPEN!
"RUGGA" RUGGA RUGGA
BRORG! BRORG! BRORG! BRORG! BRORG
WHAT IS GOING ON?
THERE'S WRITING UNDER THE JAR LID.

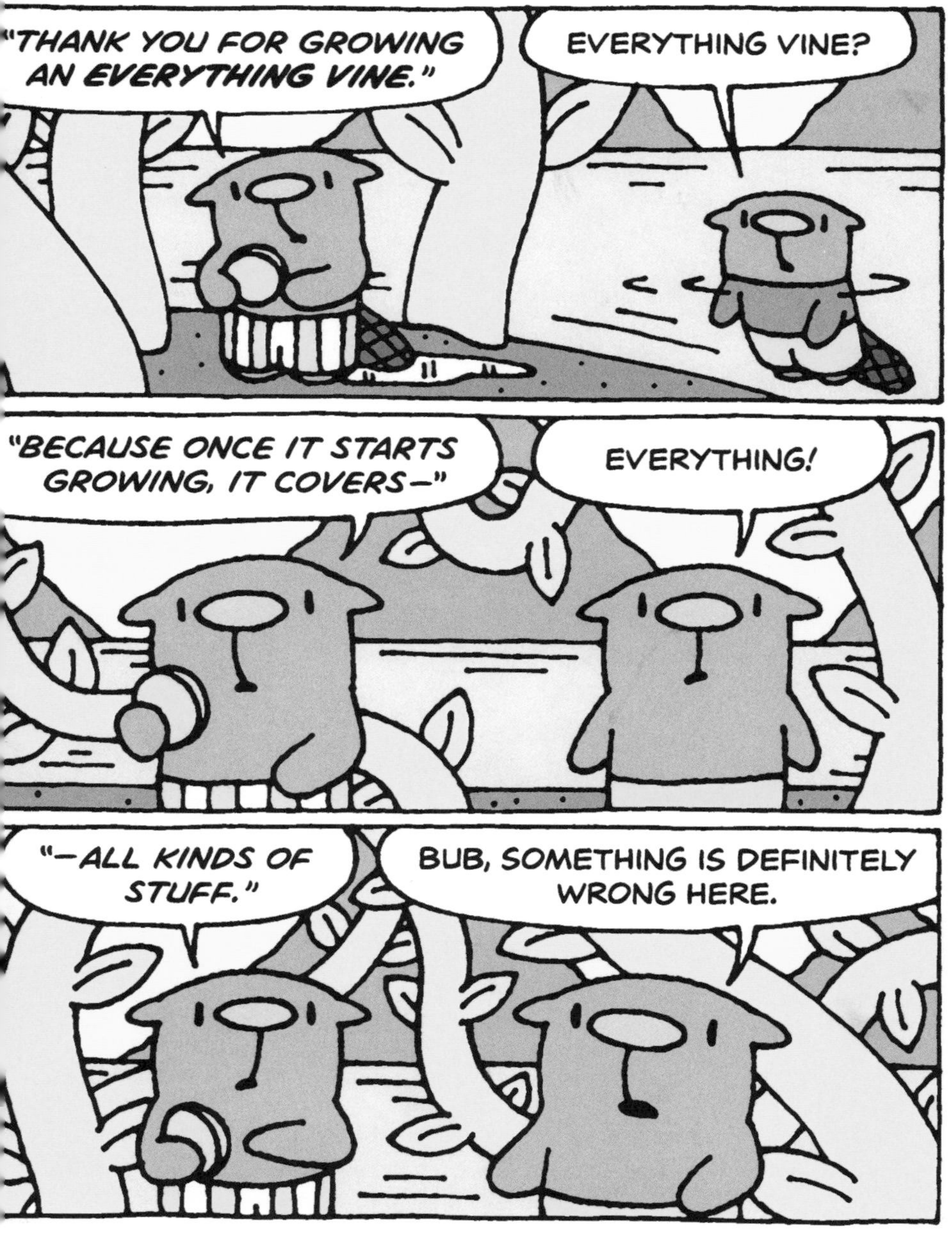
"THANK YOU FOR GROWING AN *EVERYTHING VINE.*"
EVERYTHING VINE?
"BECAUSE ONCE IT STARTS GROWING, IT COVERS—"
EVERYTHING!
"—ALL KINDS OF STUFF."
BUB, SOMETHING IS DEFINITELY WRONG HERE.

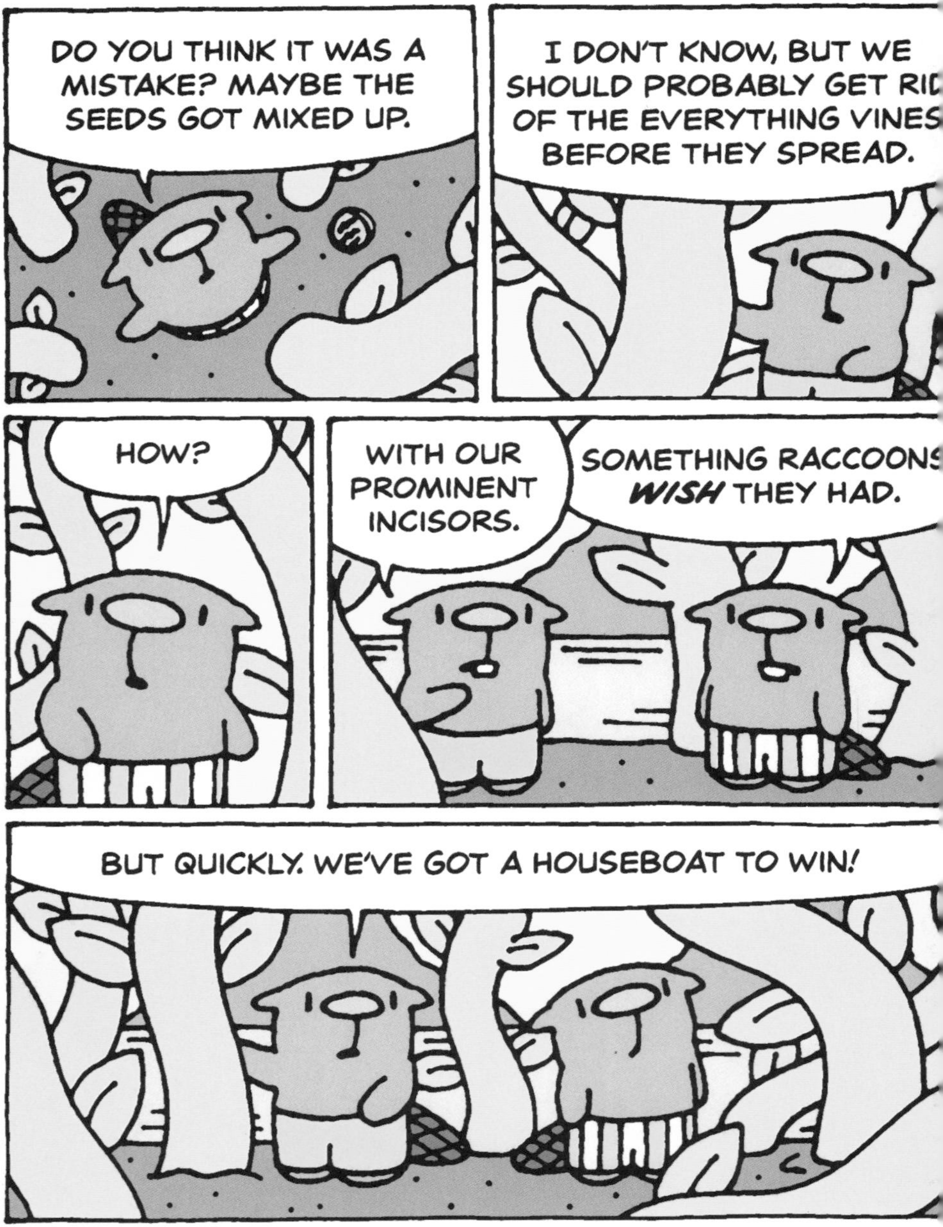
DO YOU THINK IT WAS A MISTAKE? MAYBE THE SEEDS GOT MIXED UP.
I DON'T KNOW, BUT WE SHOULD PROBABLY GET RID OF THE EVERYTHING VINES BEFORE THEY SPREAD.
HOW?
WITH OUR PROMINENT INCISORS.
SOMETHING RACCOONS *WISH* THEY HAD.
BUT QUICKLY. WE'VE GOT A HOUSEBOAT TO WIN!

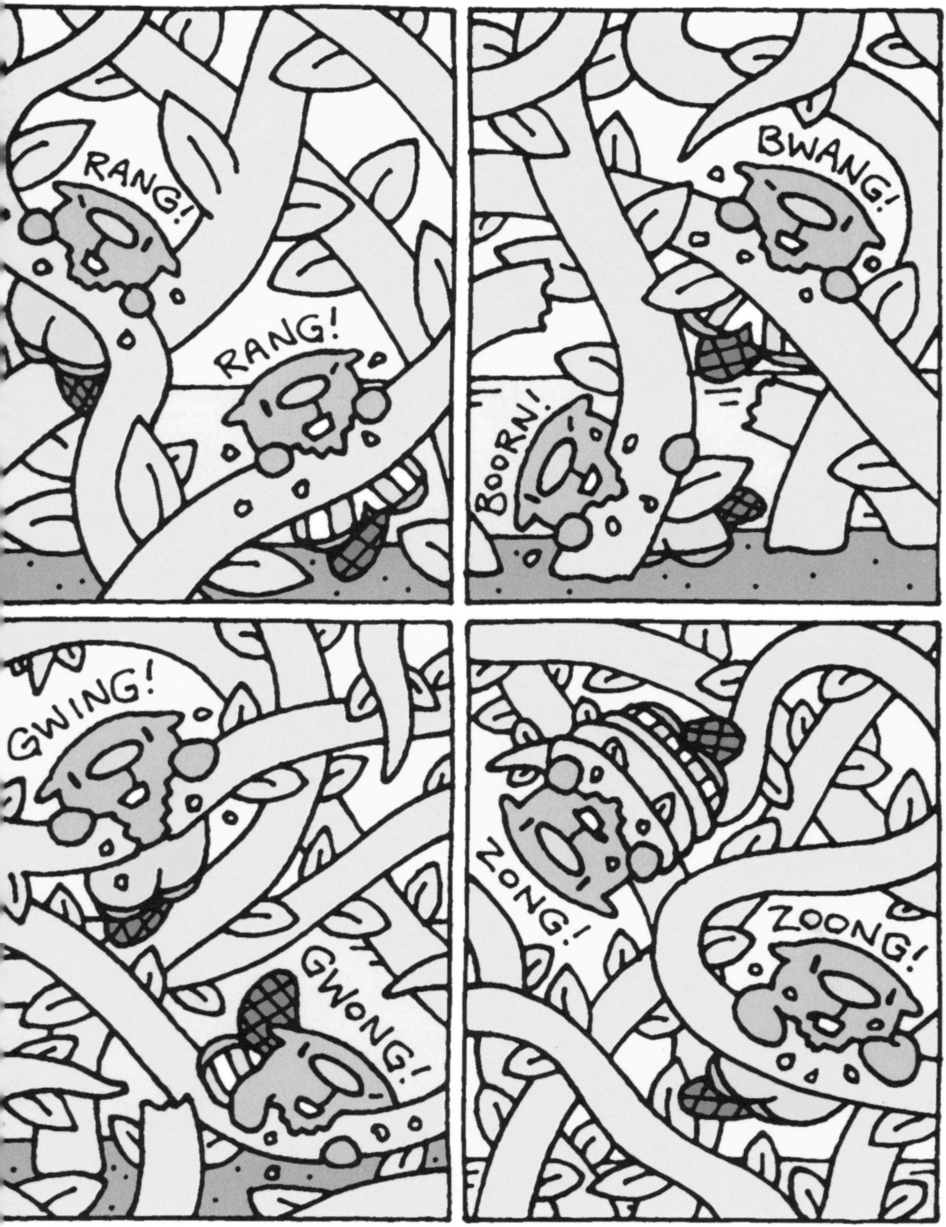
RANG!
RANG!
BWANG!
BOORN!
GWING!
GWONG!
ZONG!
ZOONG!

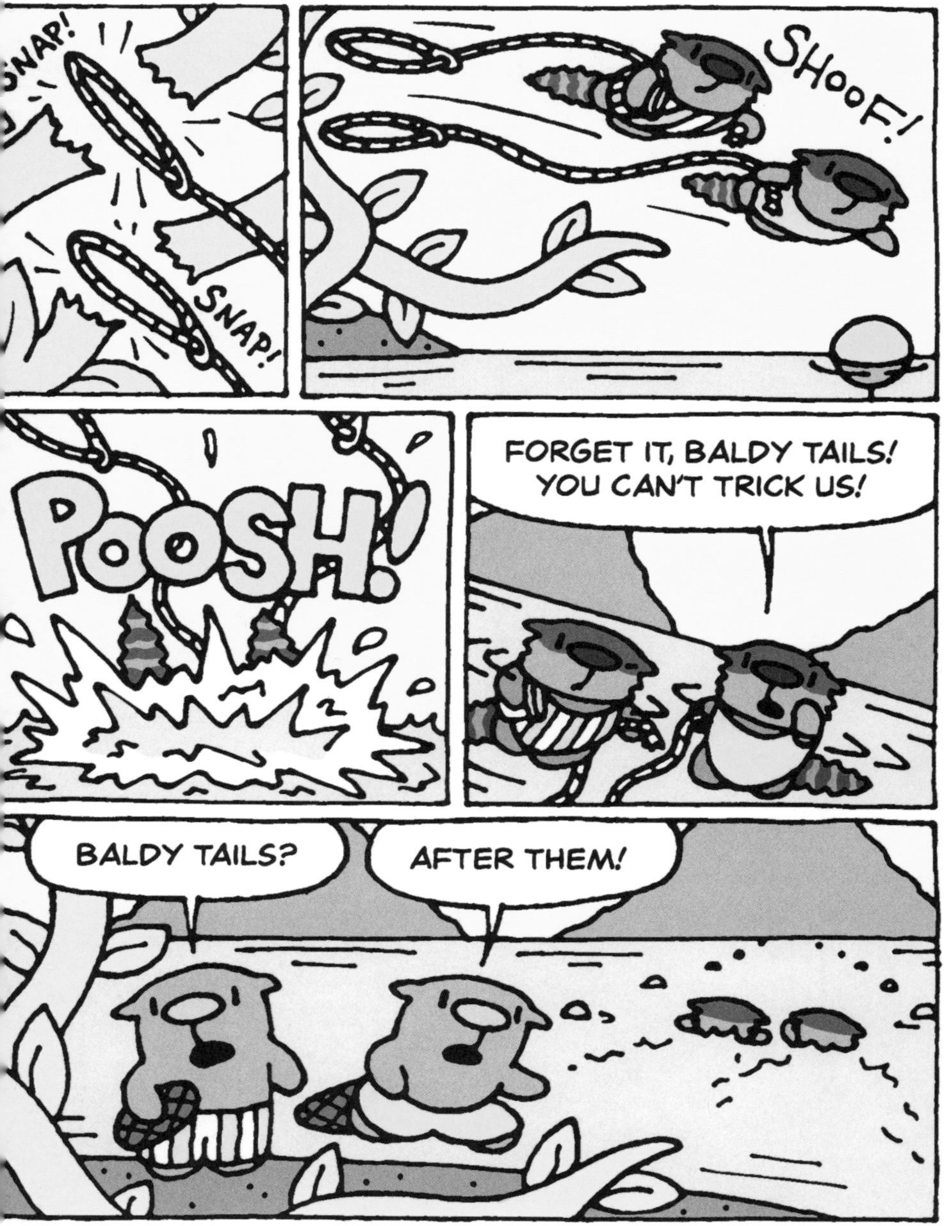
SNAP!
SNAP!
SHOOF!
POOSH!
FORGET IT, BALDY TAILS! YOU CAN'T TRICK US!
BALDY TAILS?
AFTER THEM!

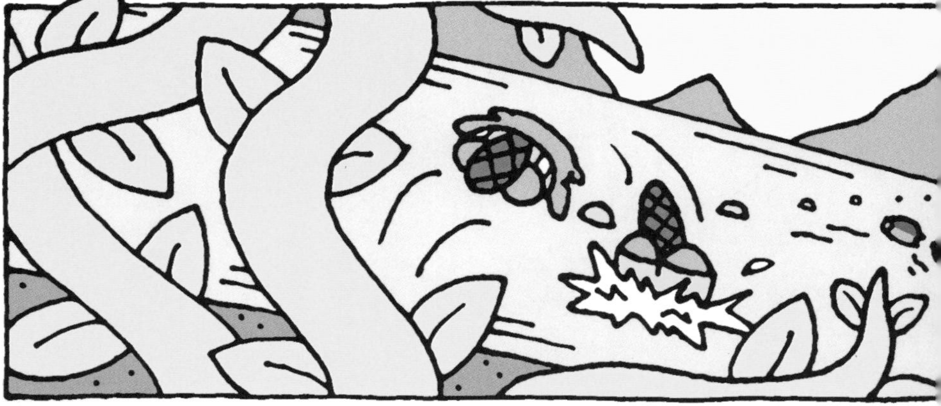

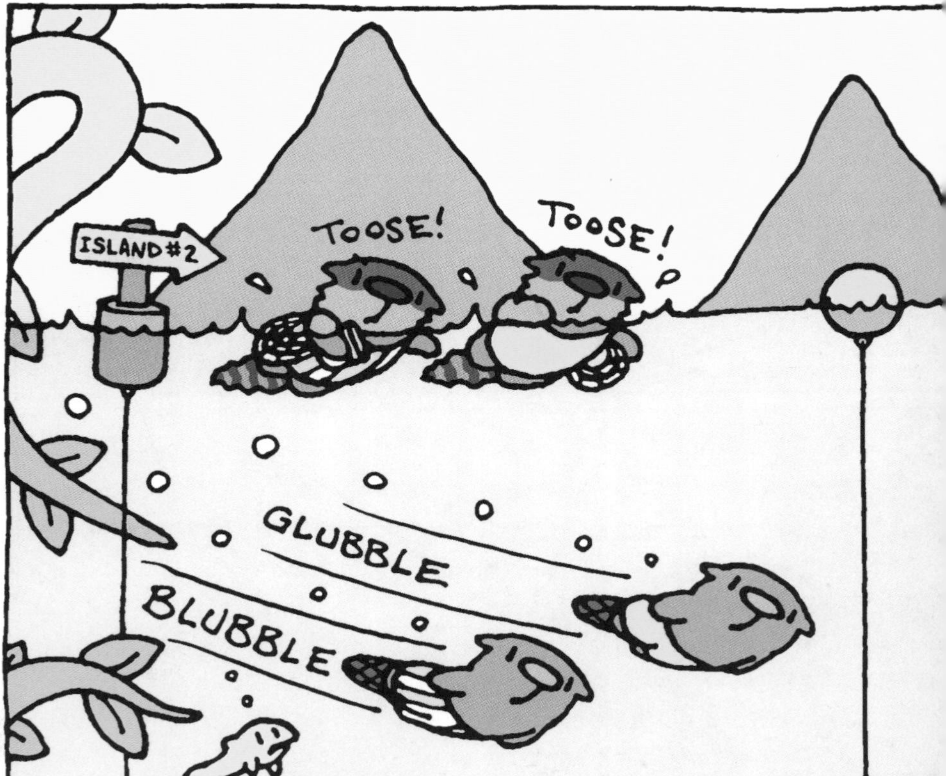
ISLAND #2
TOOSE!
TOOSE!
GLUBBLE
BLUBBLE

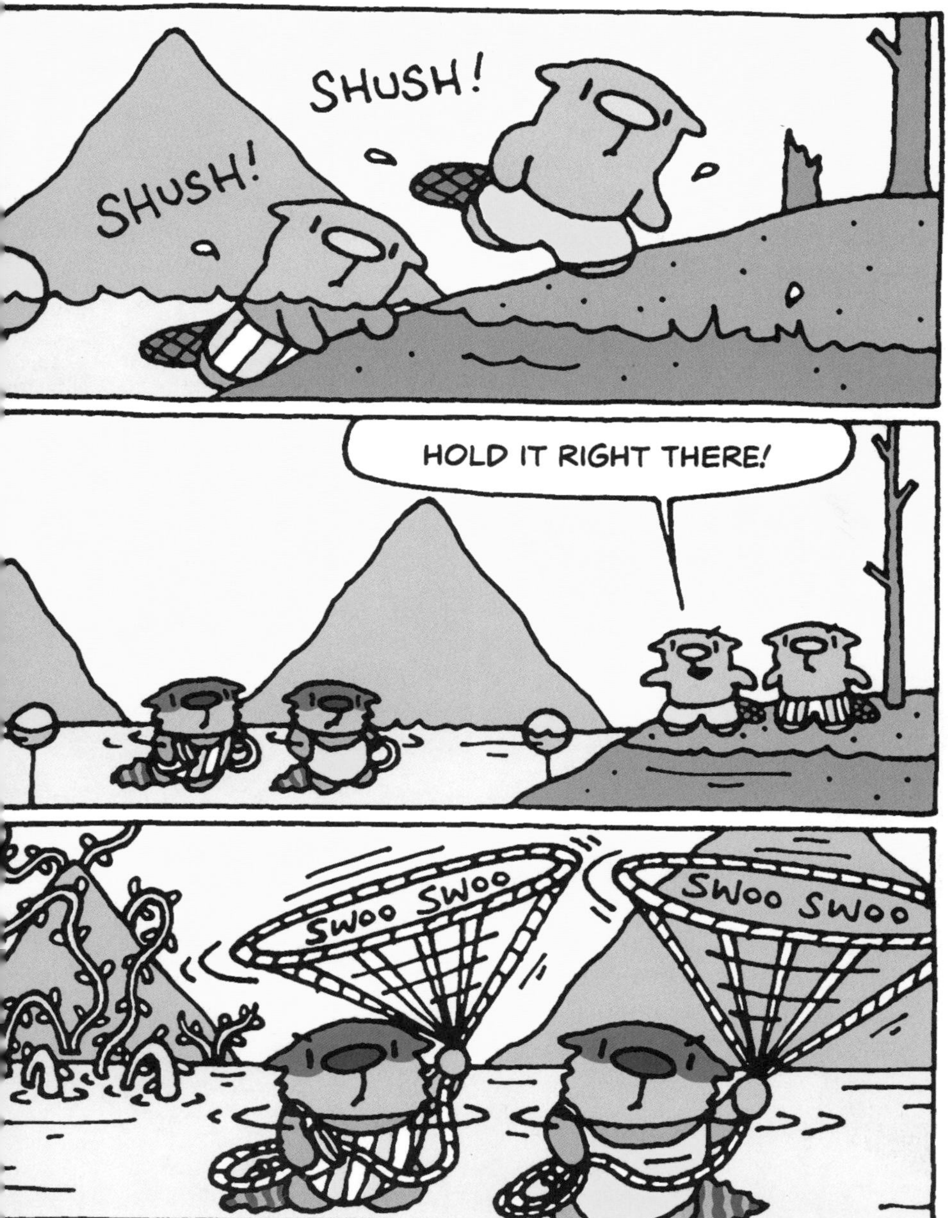
SHUSH!
SHUSH!
HOLD IT RIGHT THERE!
SWOO SWOO
SWOO SWOO

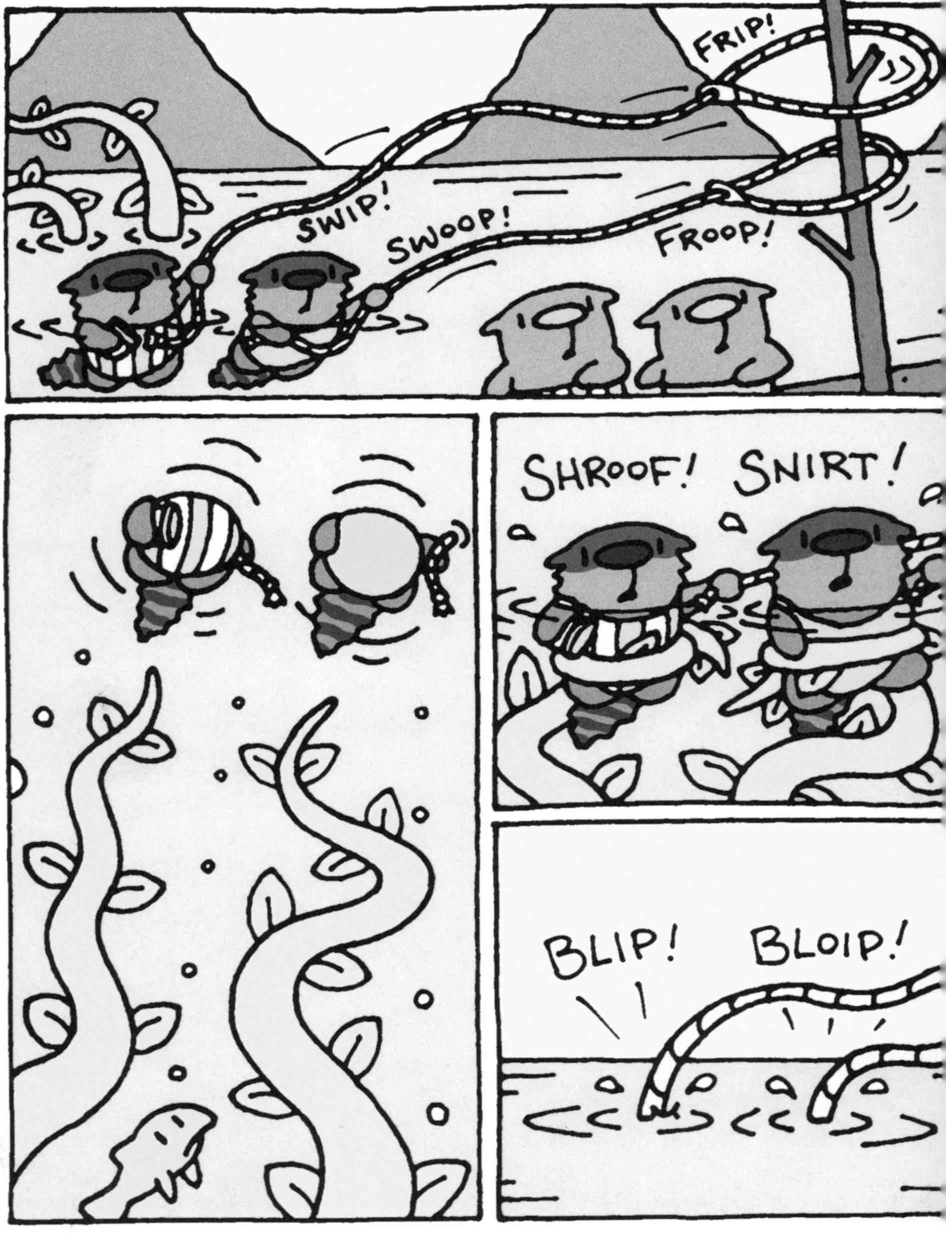
FRIP!
SWIP!
SWOOP!
FROOP!
SHROOF!
SNIRT!
BLIP!
BLOIP!

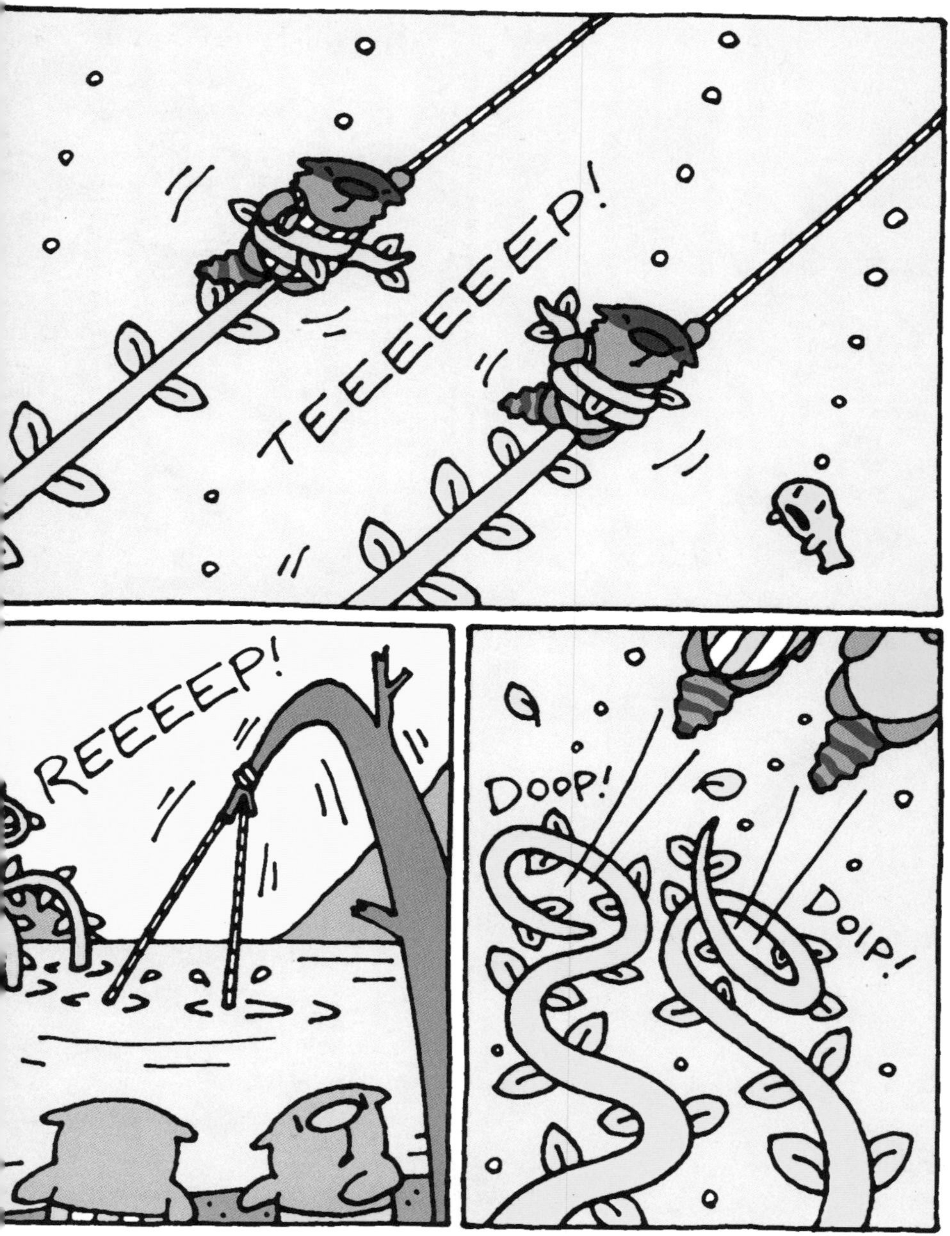
TEEEEEEEP!
REEEEEP!
DOOP!
DOIP!

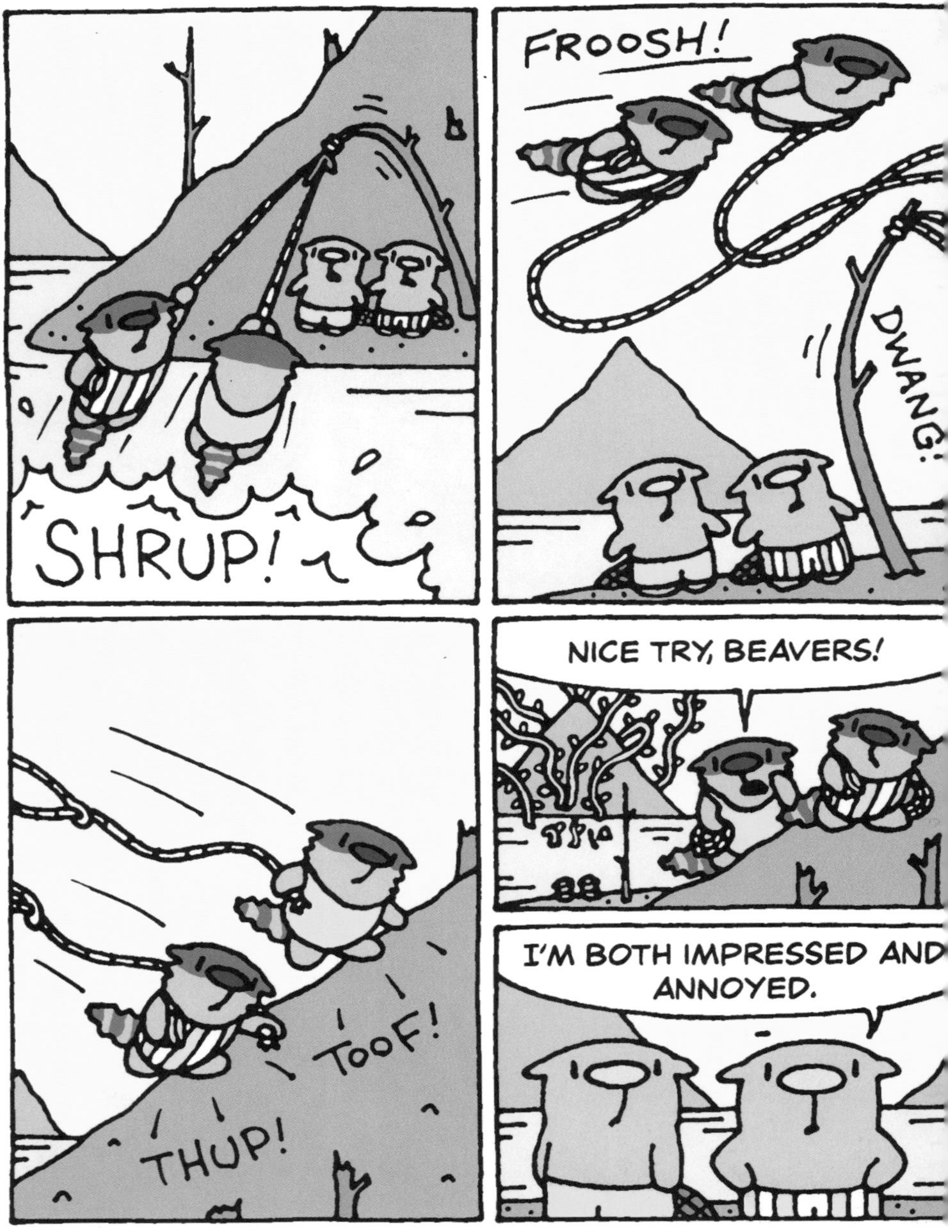
SHRUP!
FROOSH!
DWANG!
THUP!
TOOF!
NICE TRY, BEAVERS!
I'M BOTH IMPRESSED AND
ANNOYED.

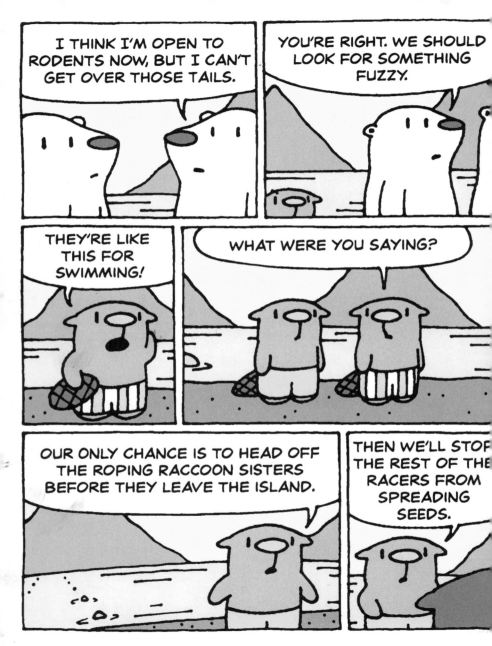

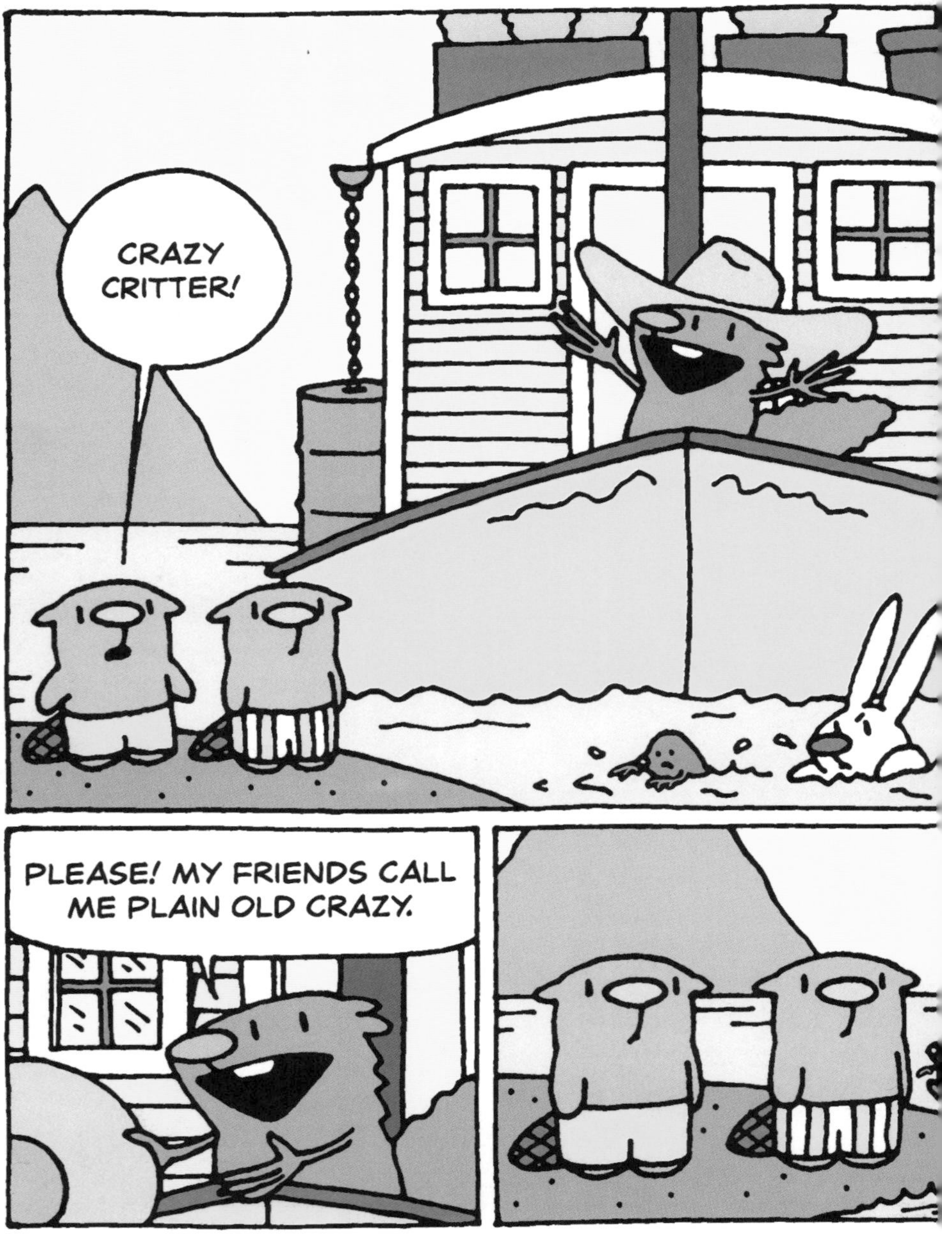
CRAZY CRITTER!
PLEASE! MY FRIENDS CALL ME PLAIN OLD CRAZY.

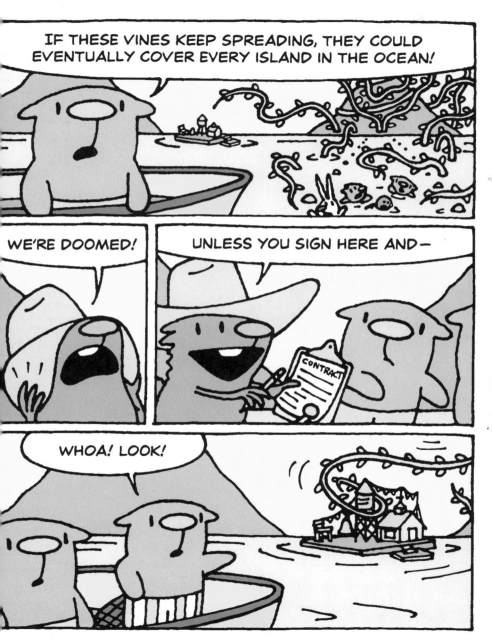

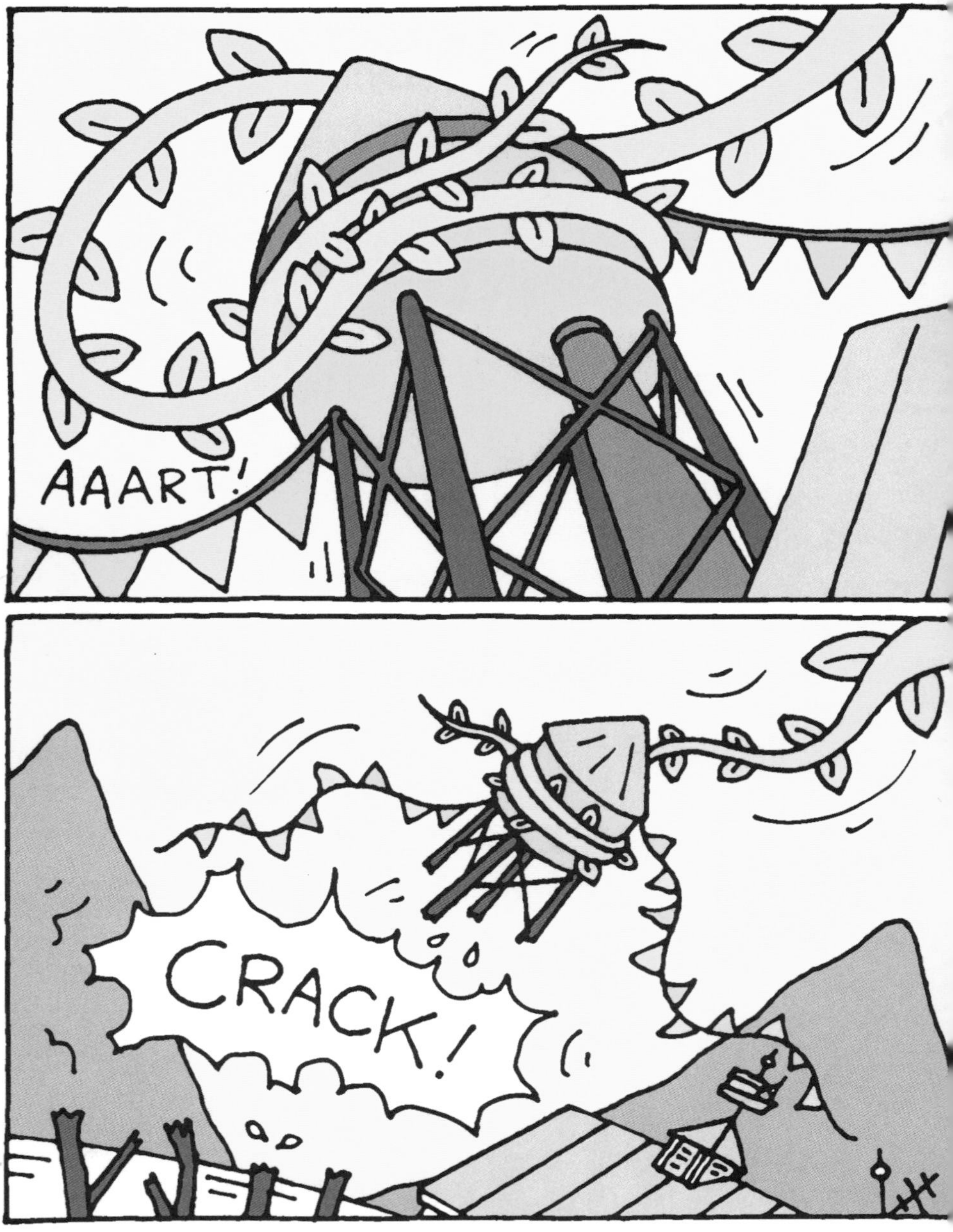
AAART!
CRACK!

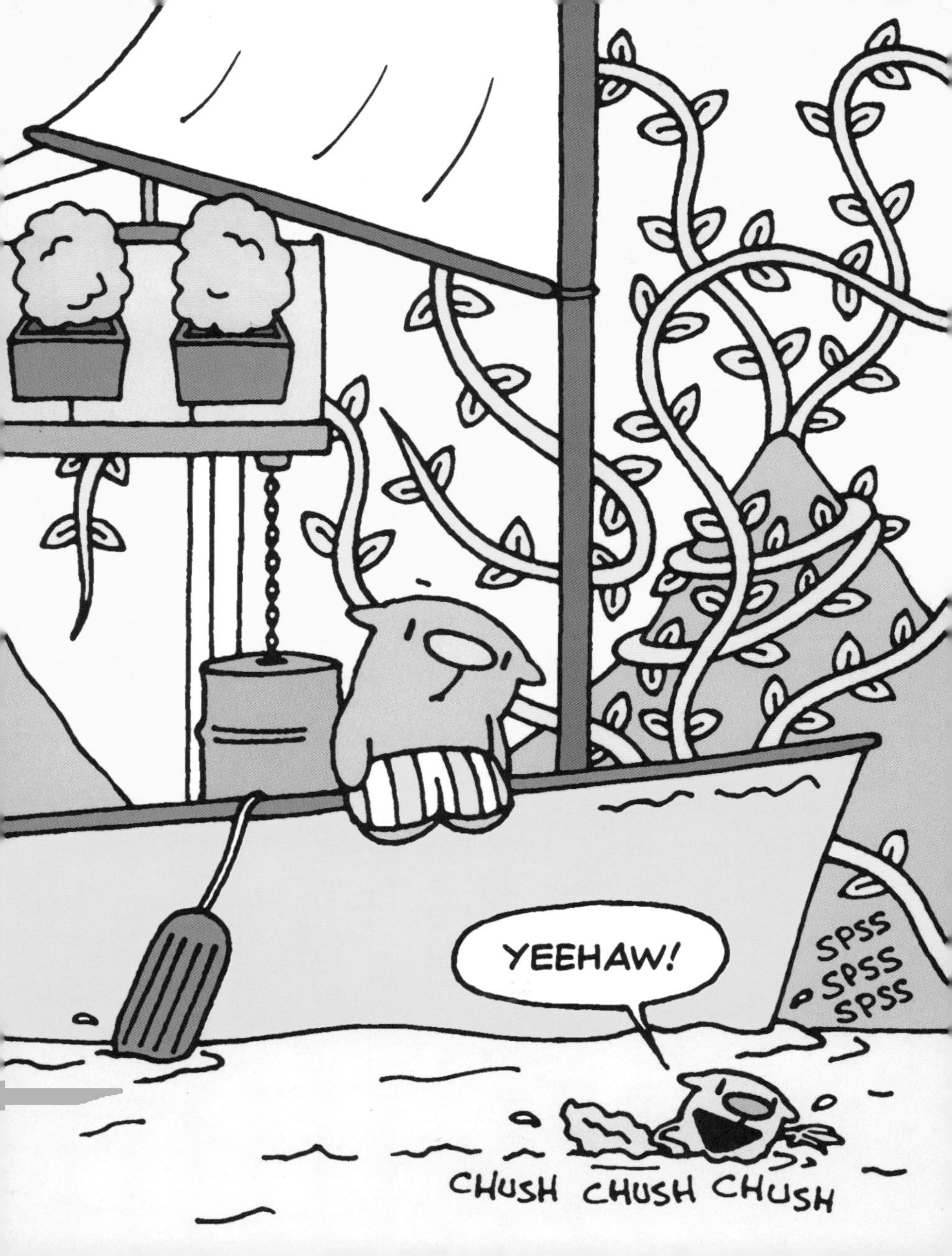
YEEHAW!
SPSS
SPSS
SPSS
CHUSH CHUSH CHUSH

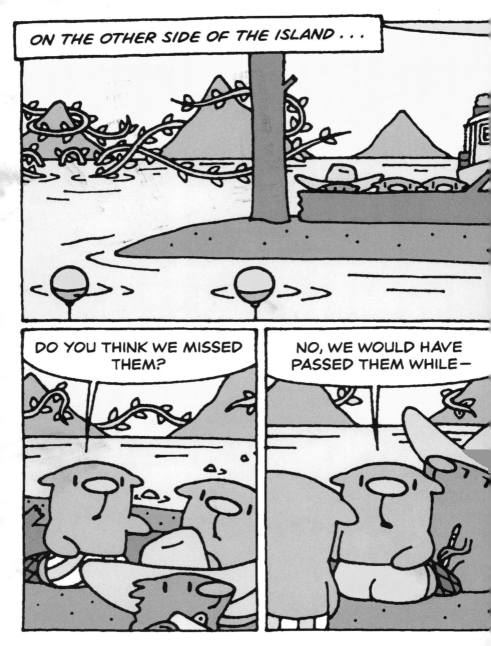

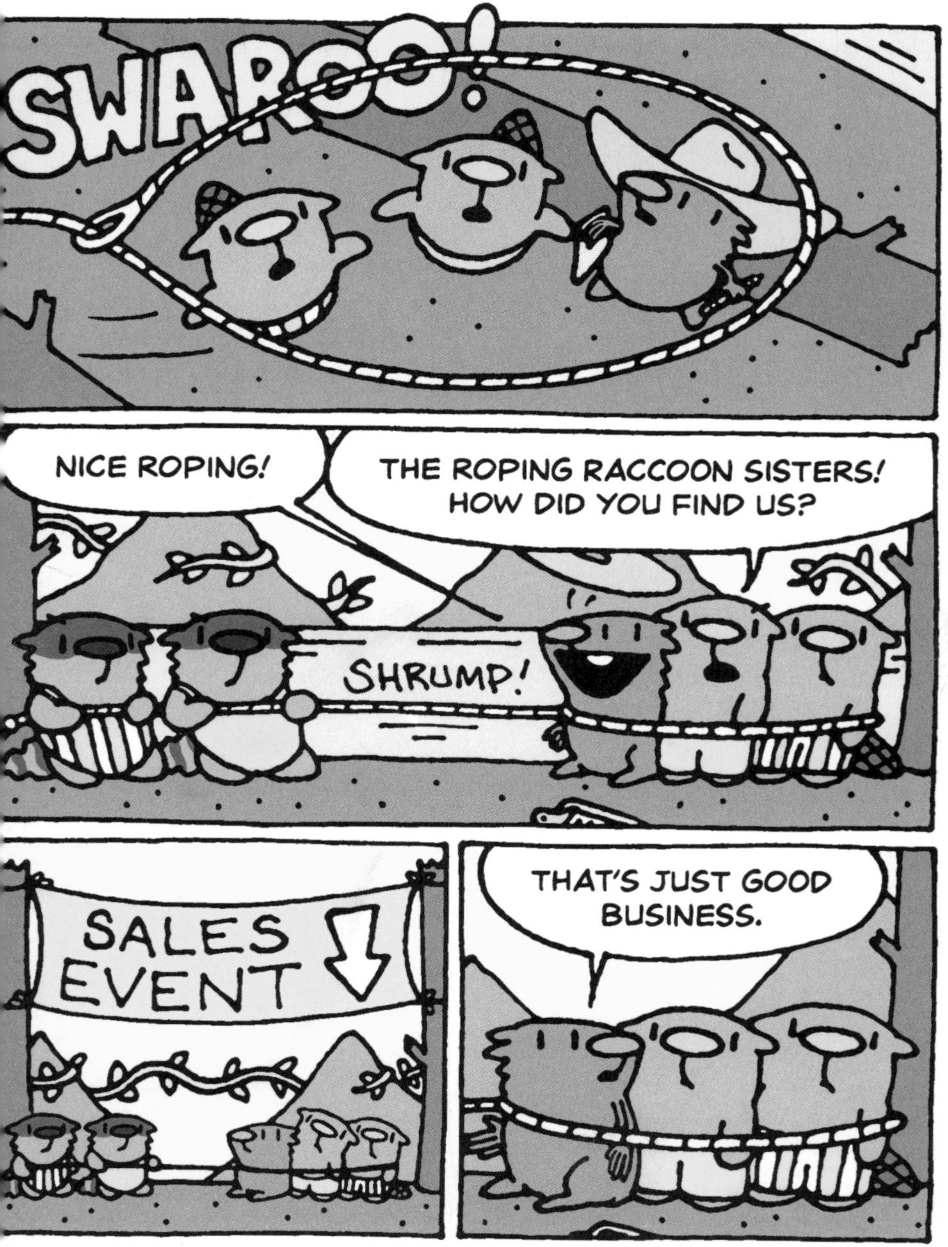
SWAROO!
NICE ROPING!
THE ROPING RACCOON SISTERS! HOW DID YOU FIND US?
SHRUMP!
SALES EVENT
THAT'S JUST GOOD BUSINESS.

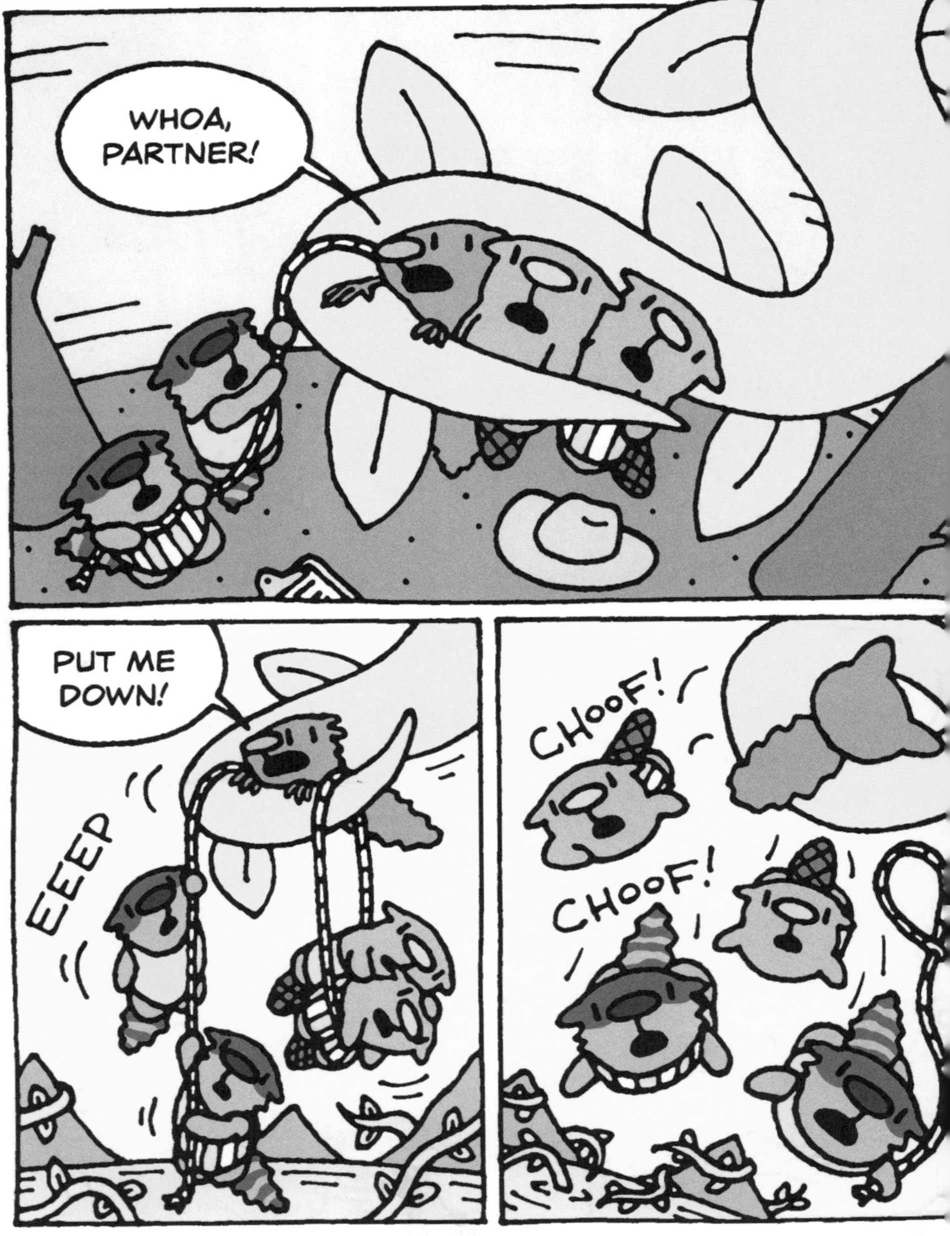
WHOA, PARTNER!
PUT ME DOWN!
EEEEP
CHOOF!
CHOOF!

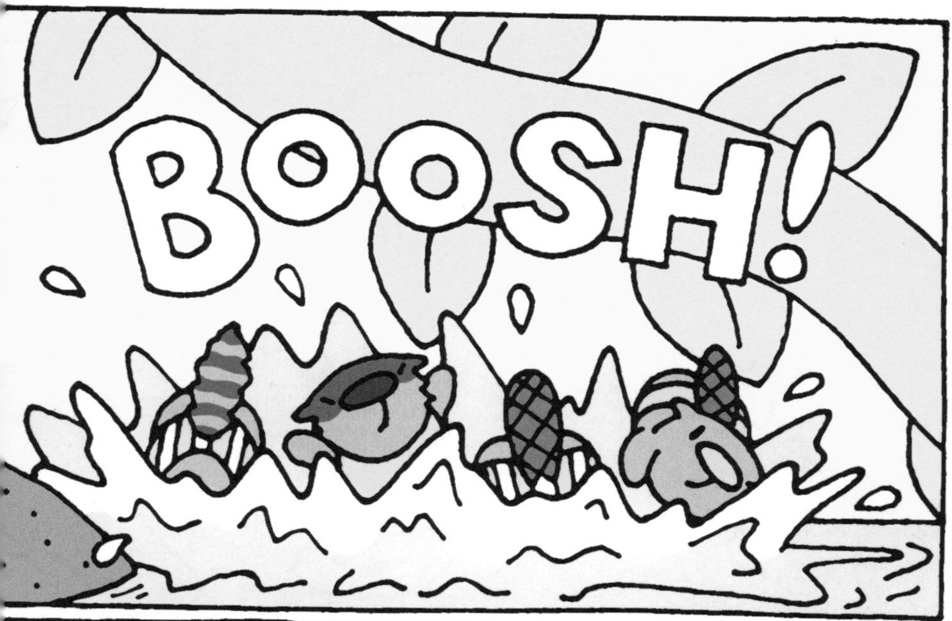
BOOSH!

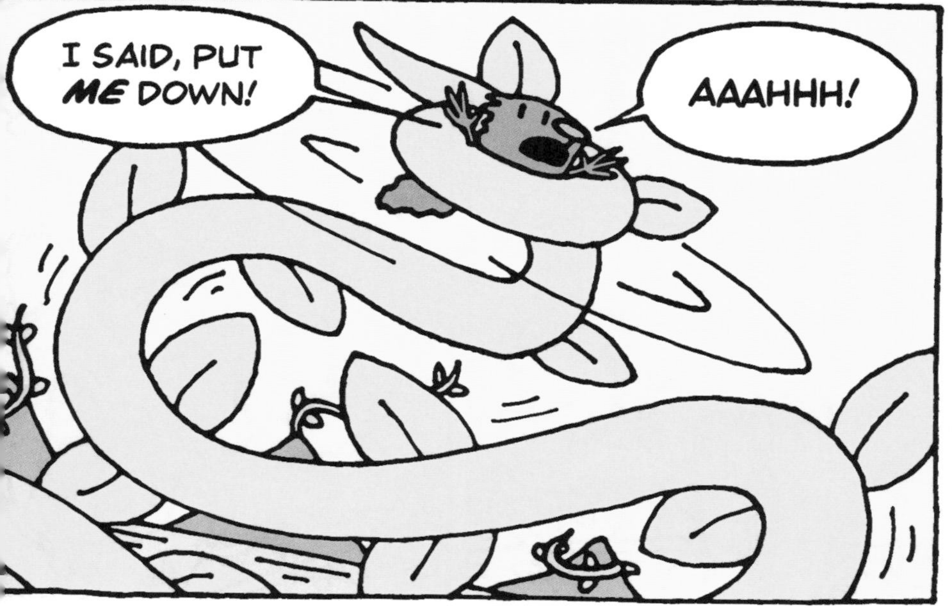
I SAID, PUT *ME* DOWN!
AAAHHH!

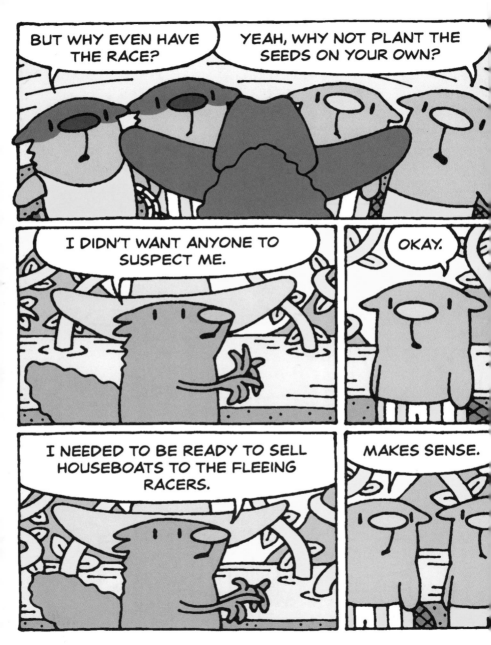

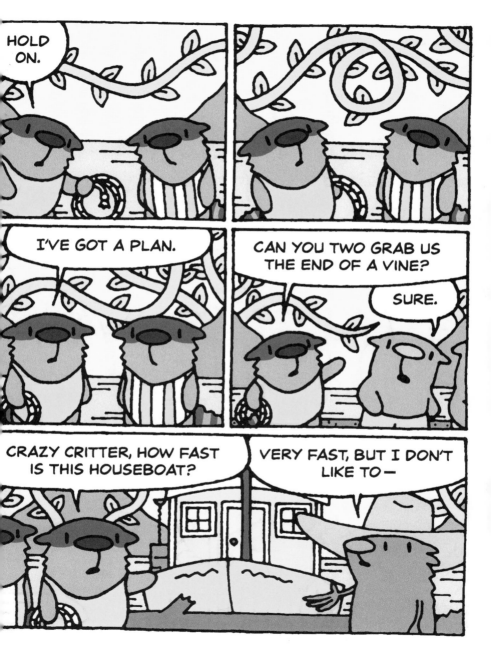

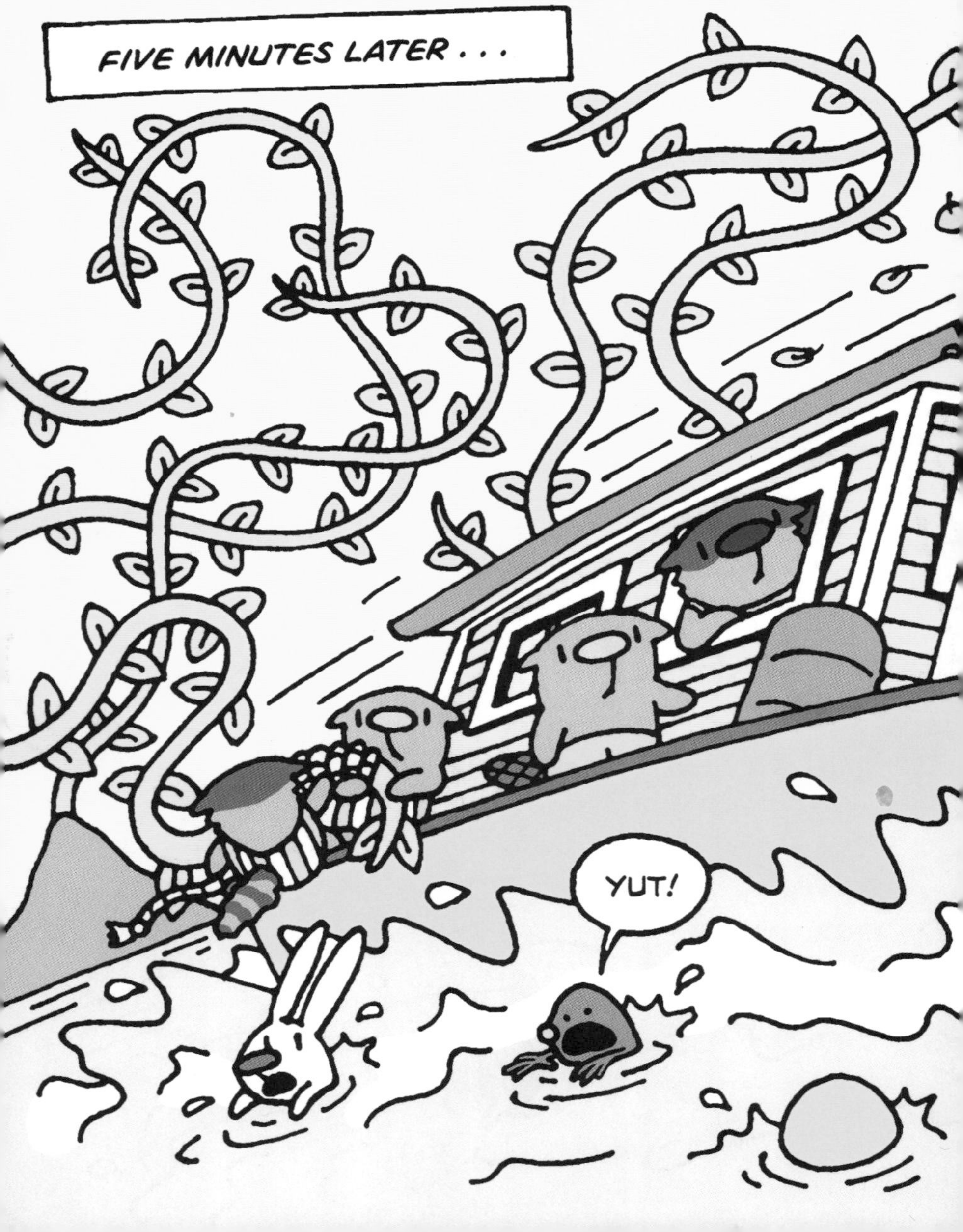
FIVE MINUTES LATER . . .
YUT!

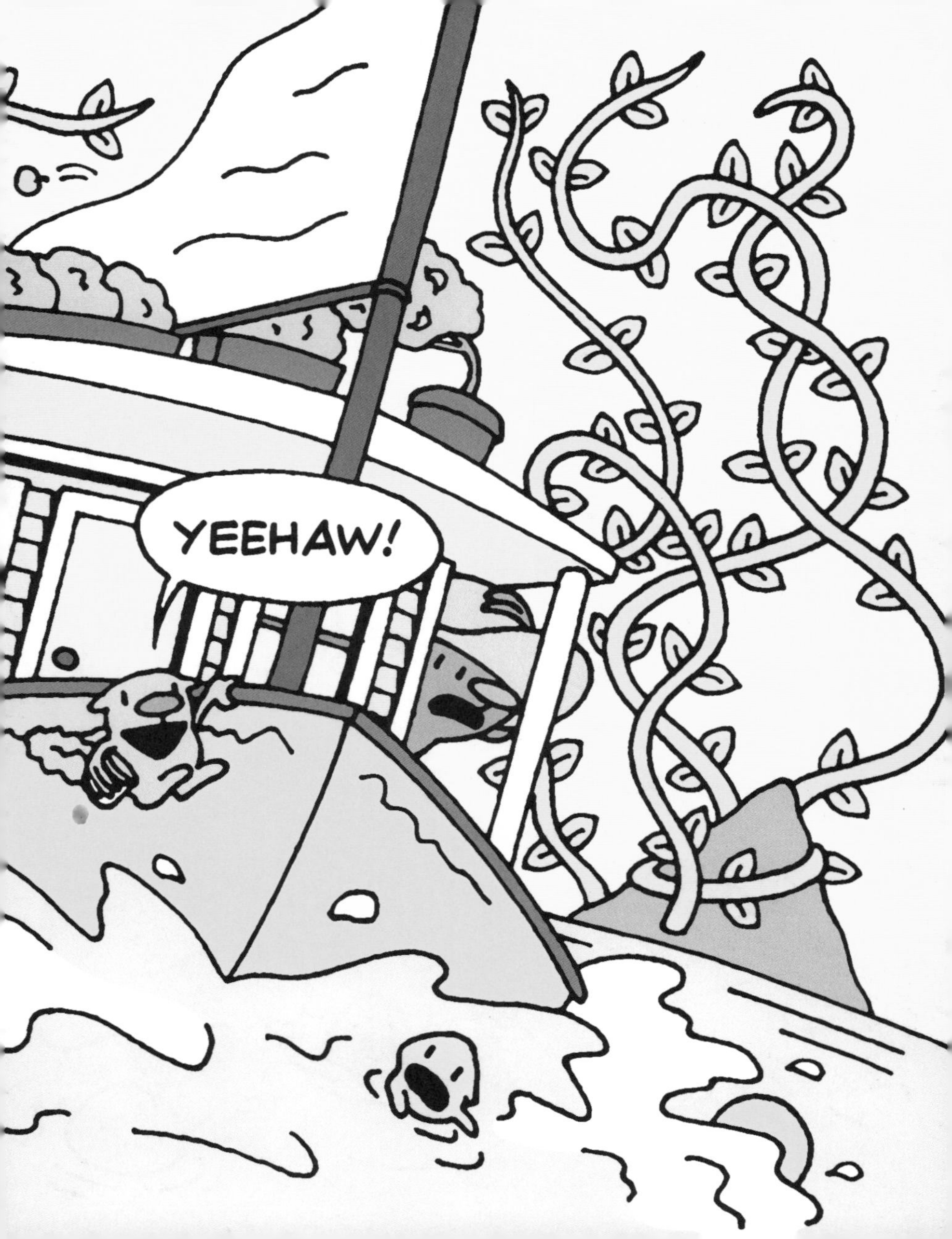
YEEHAW!

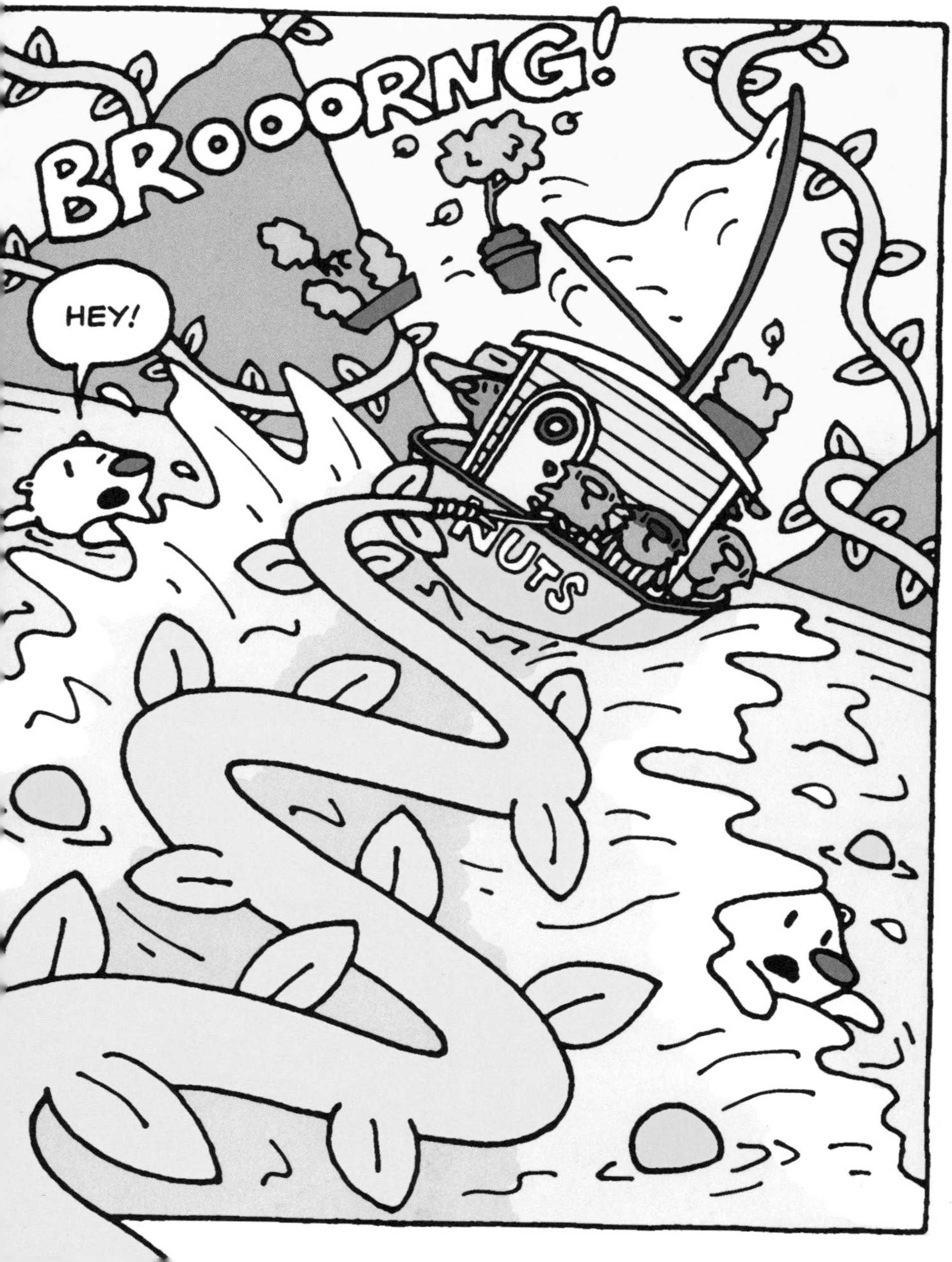
BROOORNG!
HEY!
NUTS

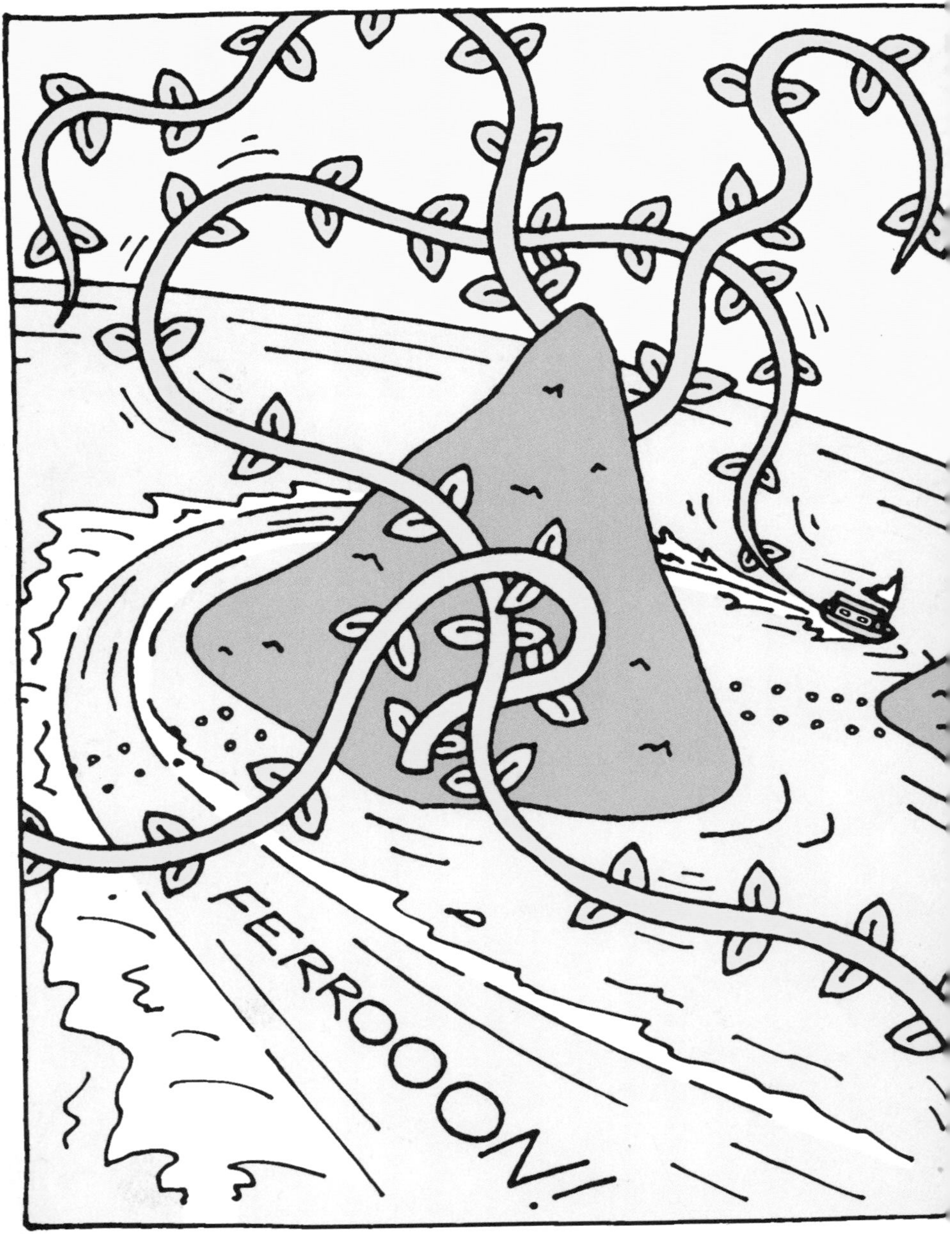
FERROOOON!

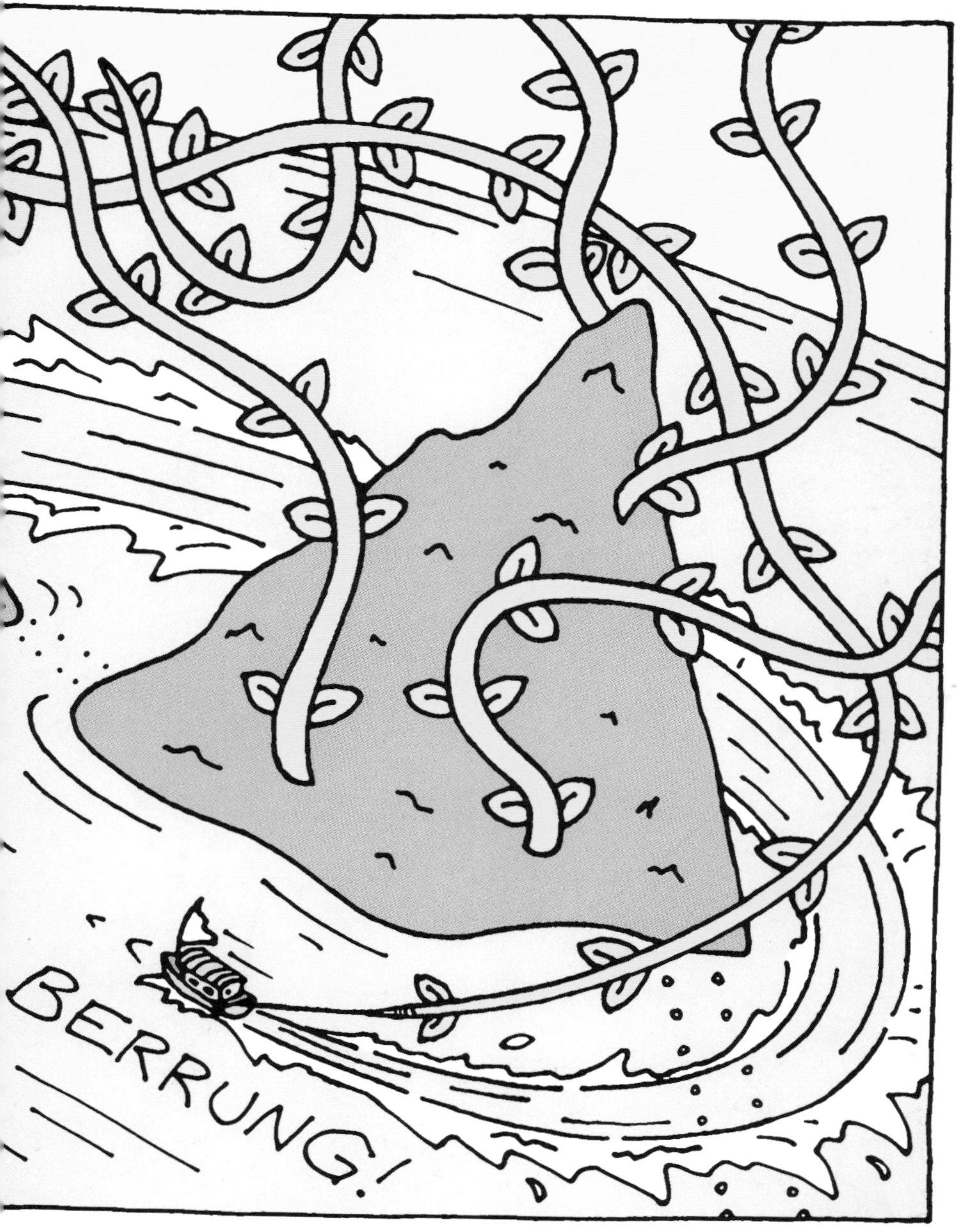
BERRUNG!

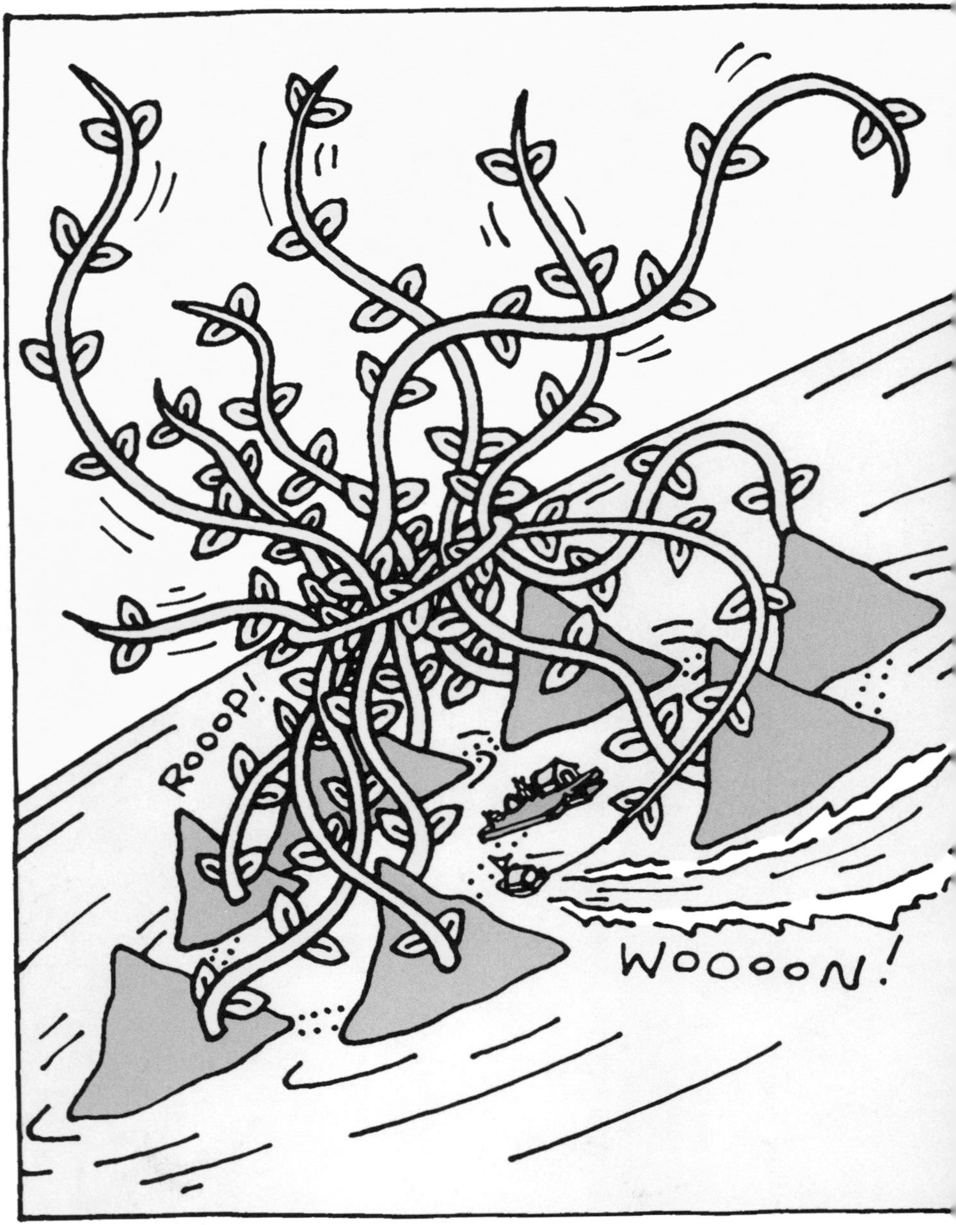

Rooop!
WOOOON!

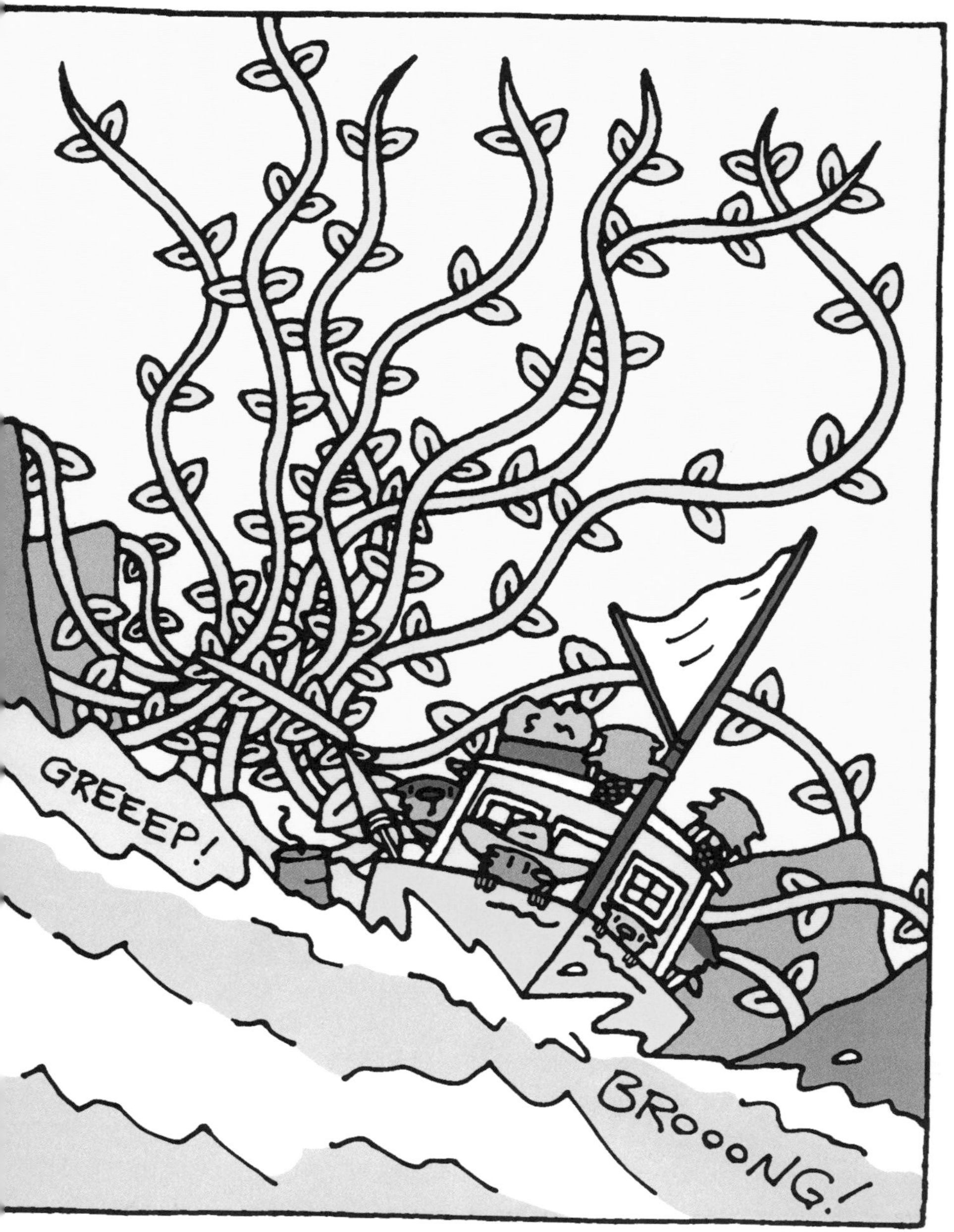

GREEEEP!
BROOONG!

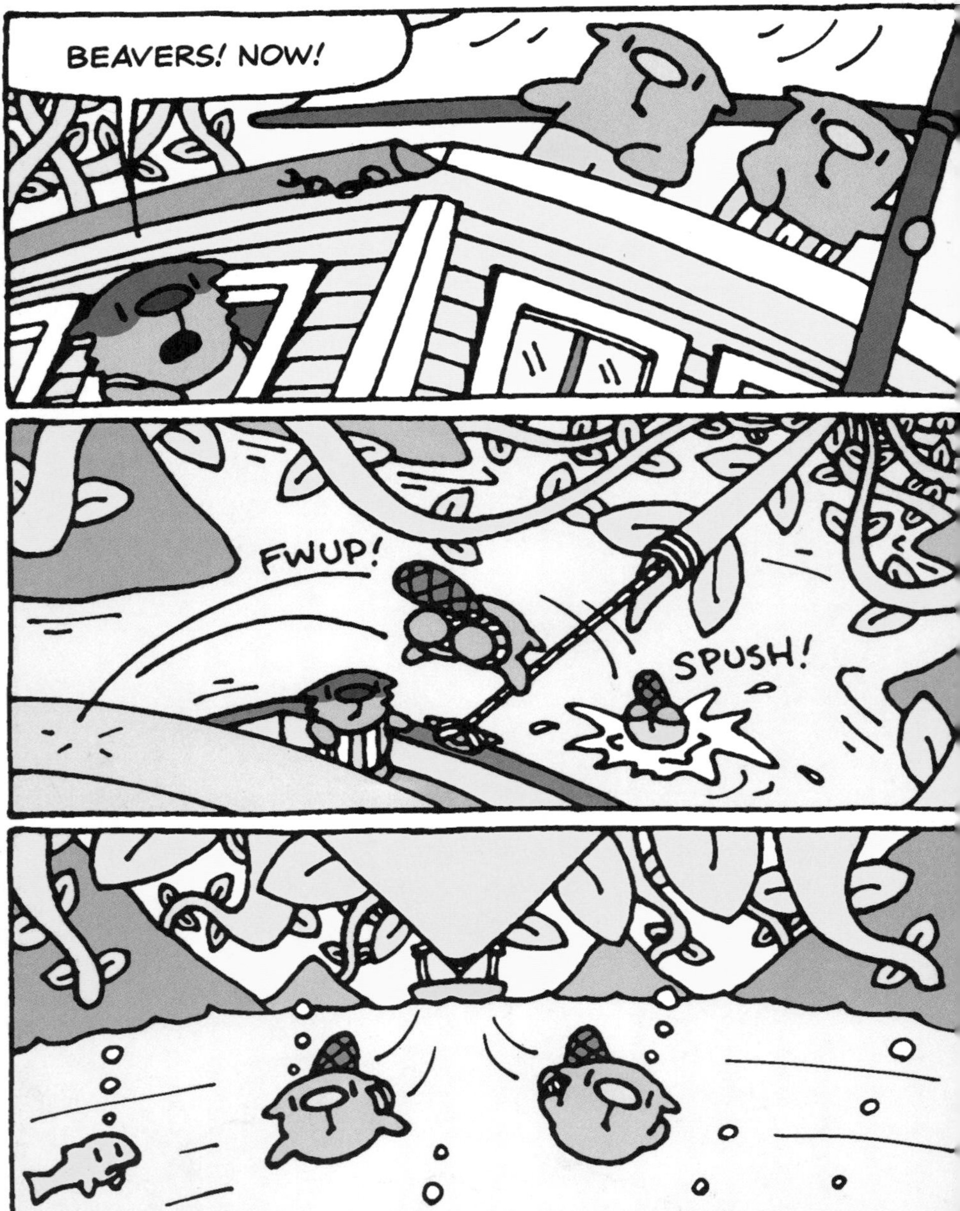
BEAVERS! NOW!
FWUP!
SPUSH!

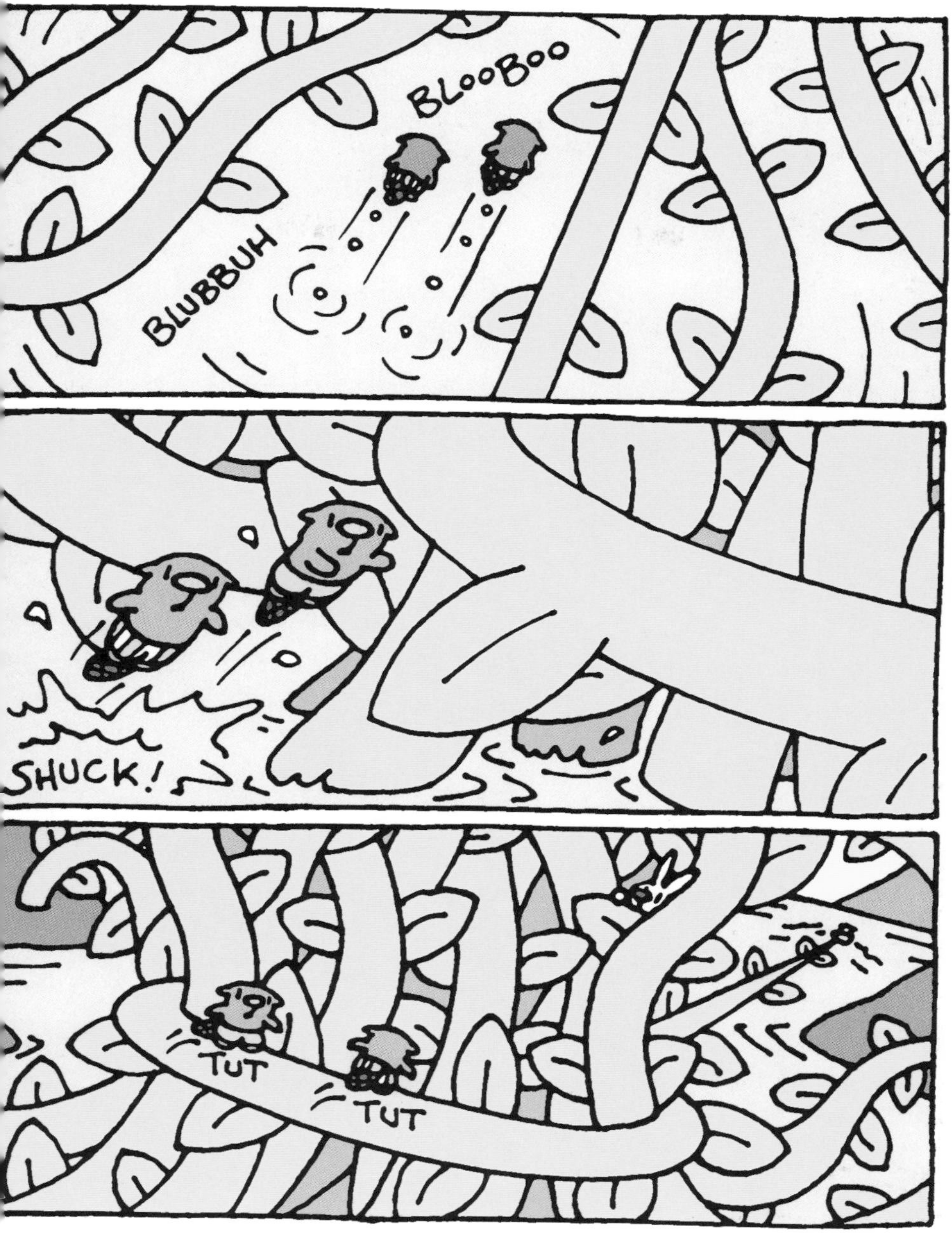
BLOOBOO
BLUBBUH
SHUCK!
TUT
TUT

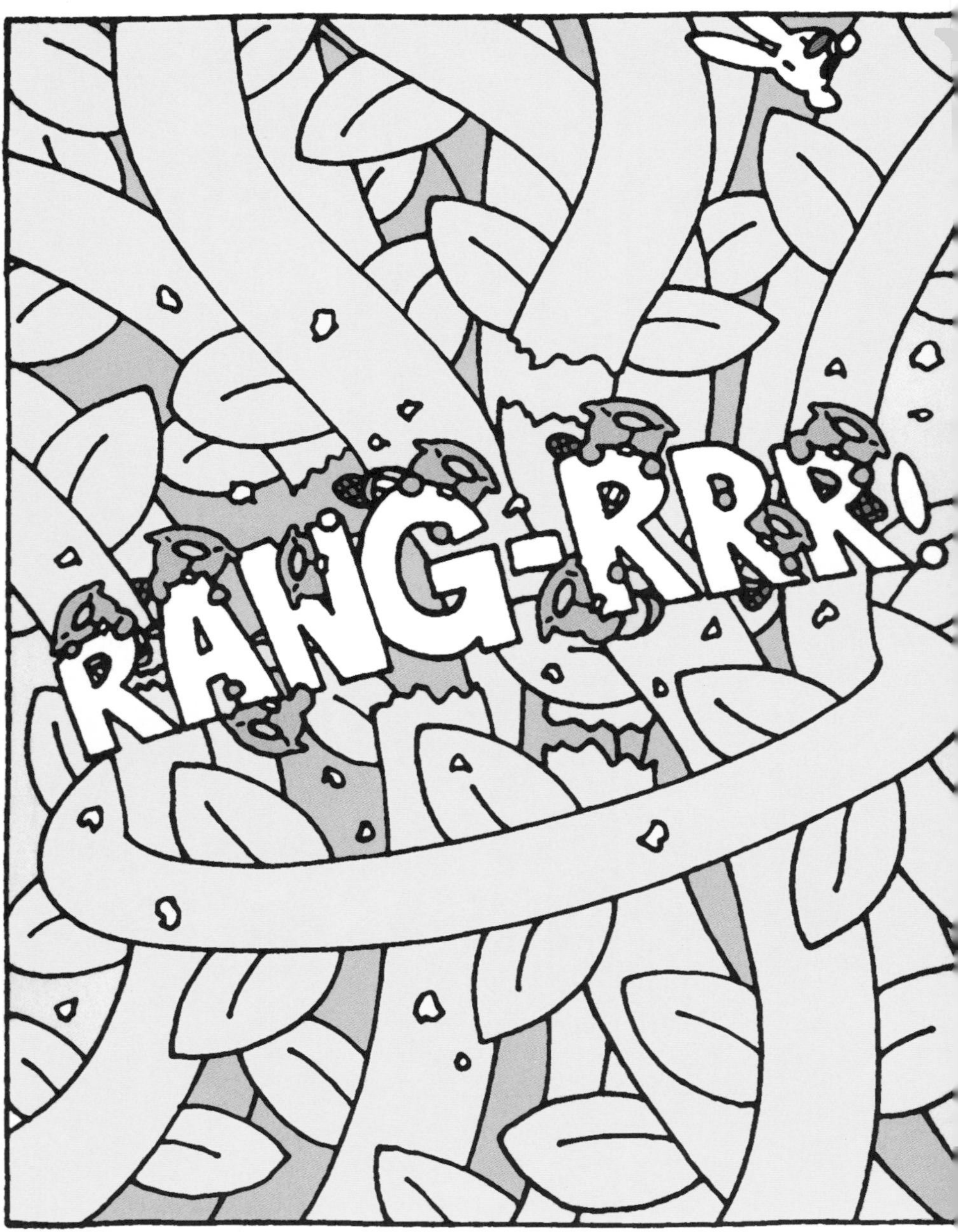
RANG-RRR!

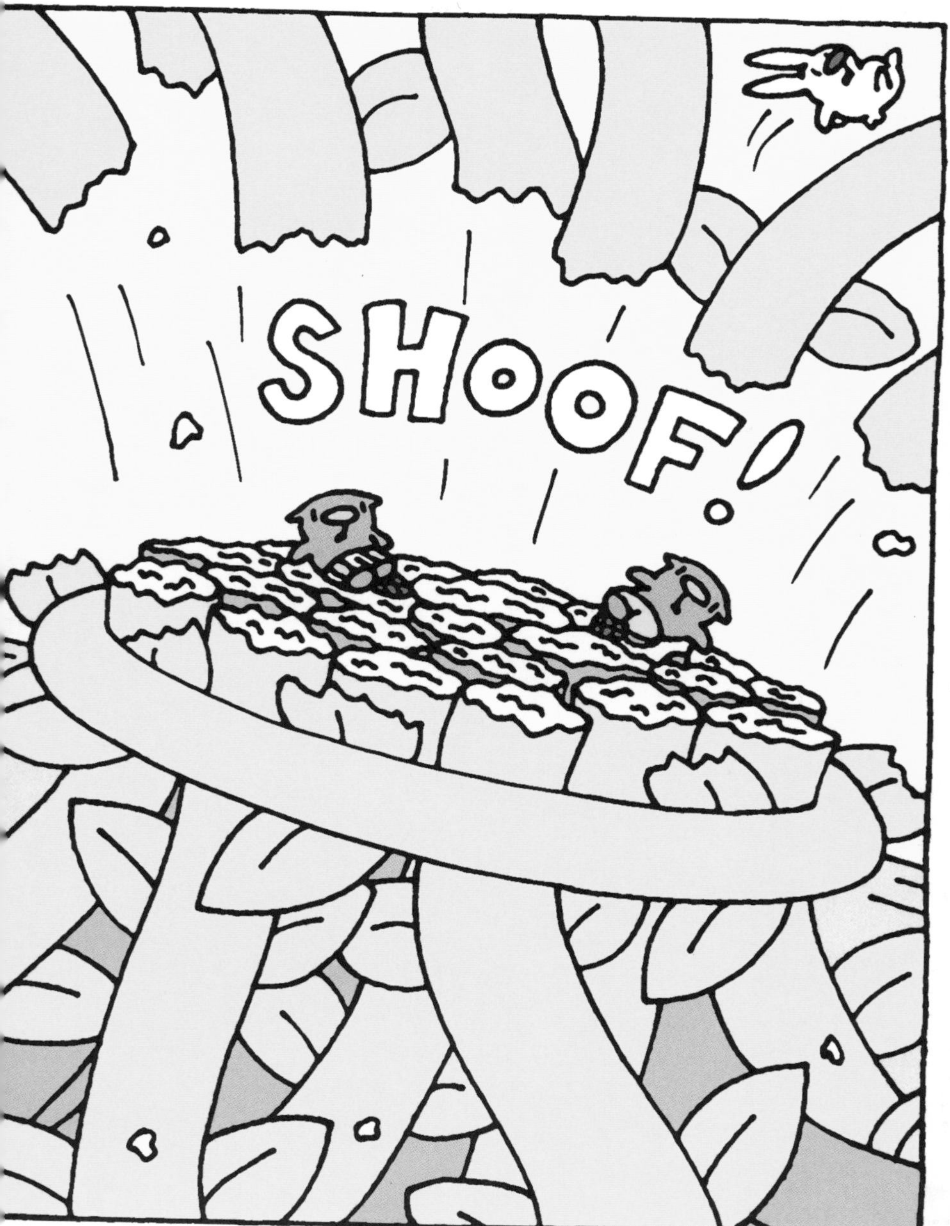
SHOOF!

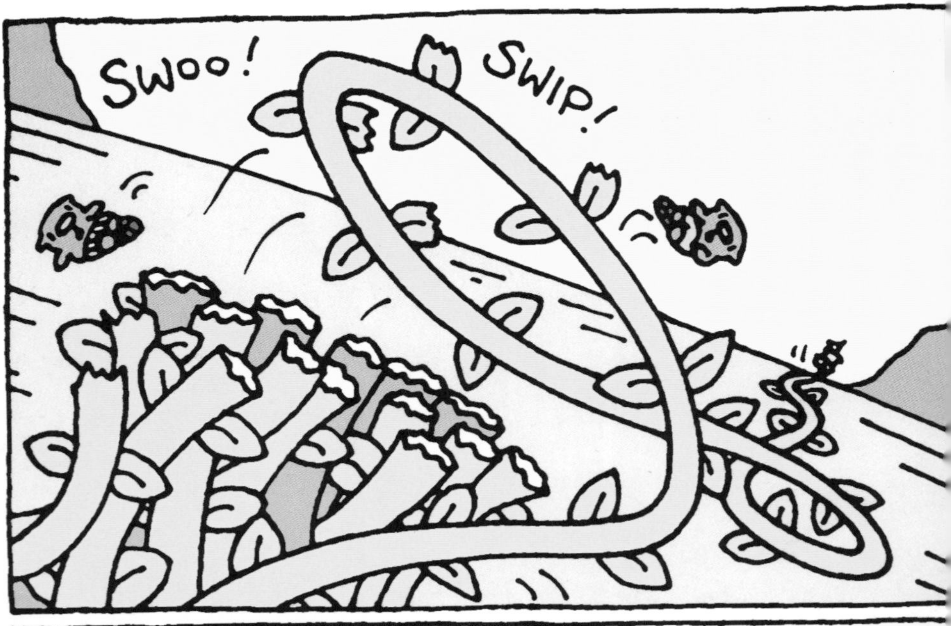
SWOO!
SWIP!

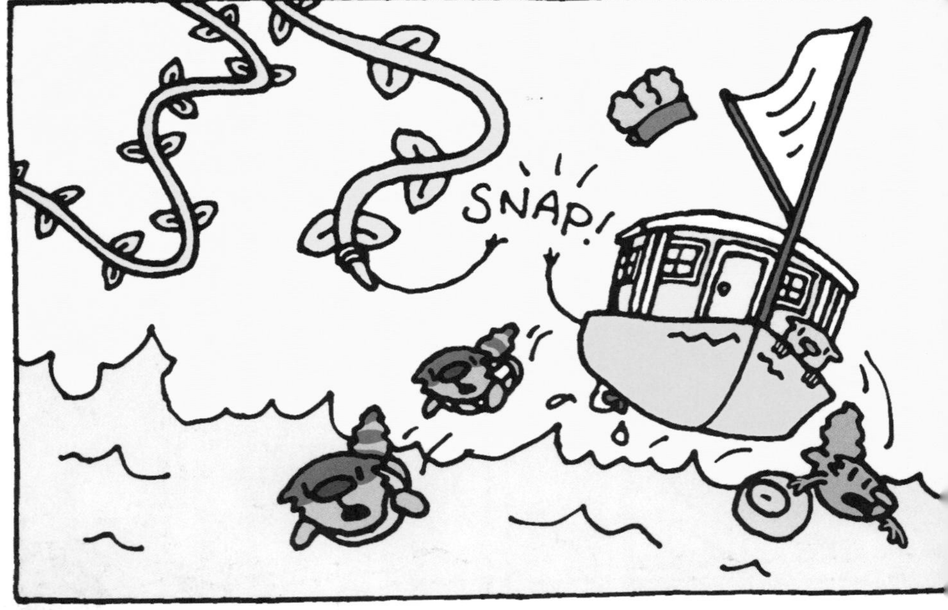
SNAP!

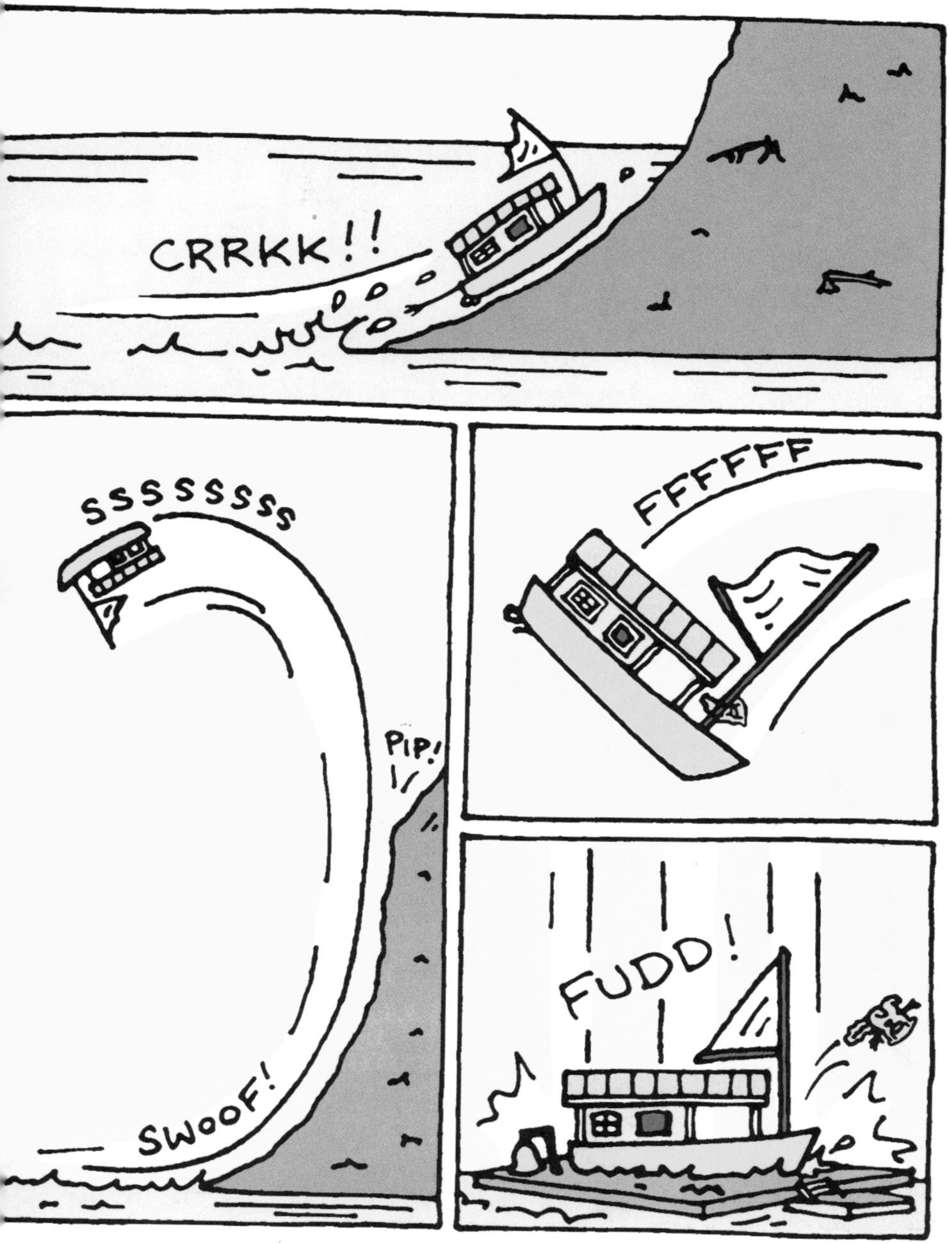
CRRKK!!
SSSSSSSSS
PIP!
SWOOF!
FFFFFF
FUDD!

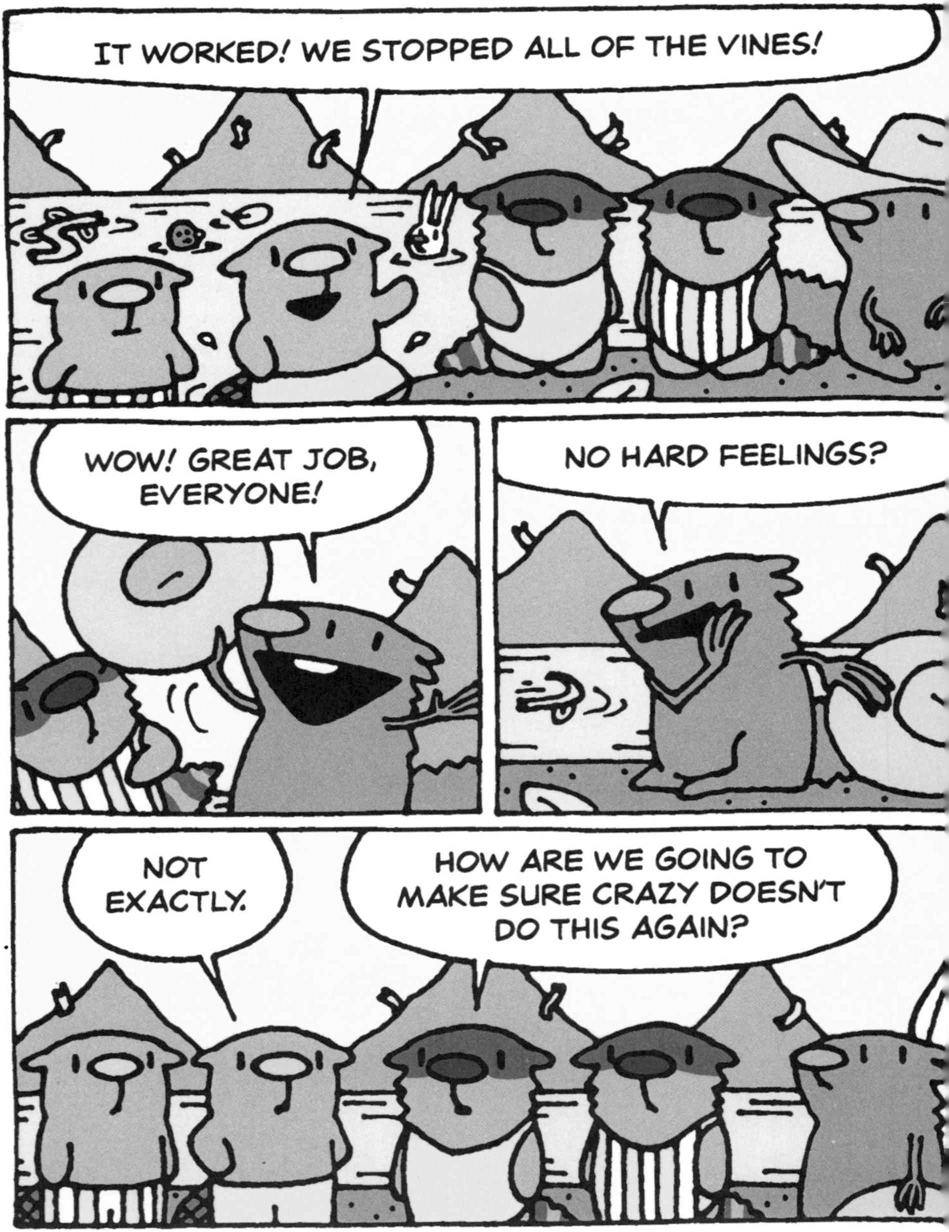

IT WORKED! WE STOPPED ALL OF THE VINES!
WOW! GREAT JOB, EVERYONE!
NO HARD FEELINGS?
NOT EXACTLY.
HOW ARE WE GOING TO MAKE SURE CRAZY DOESN'T DO THIS AGAIN?

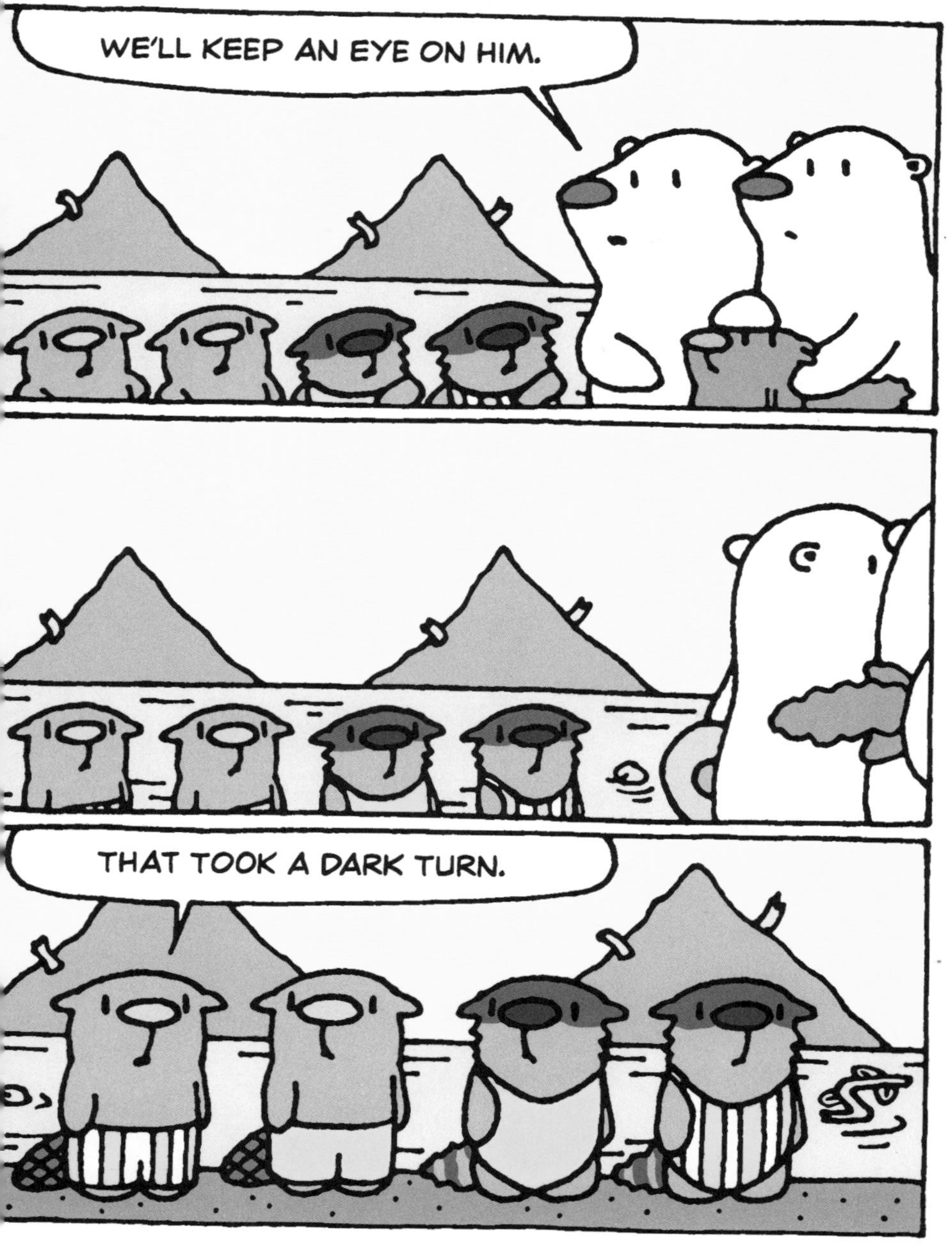
WE'LL KEEP AN EYE ON HIM.
THAT TOOK A DARK TURN.

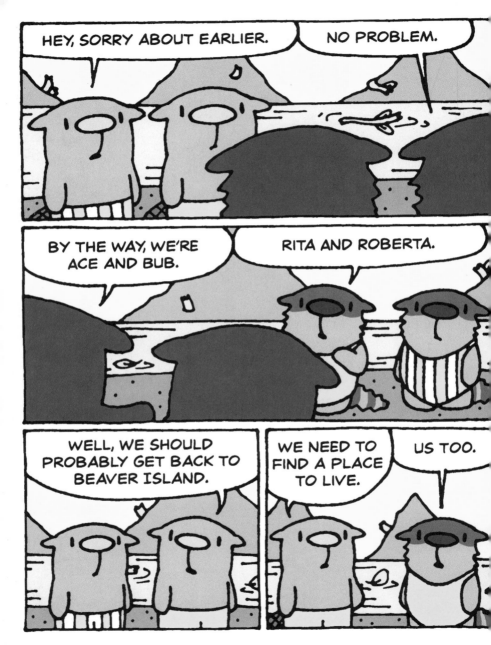

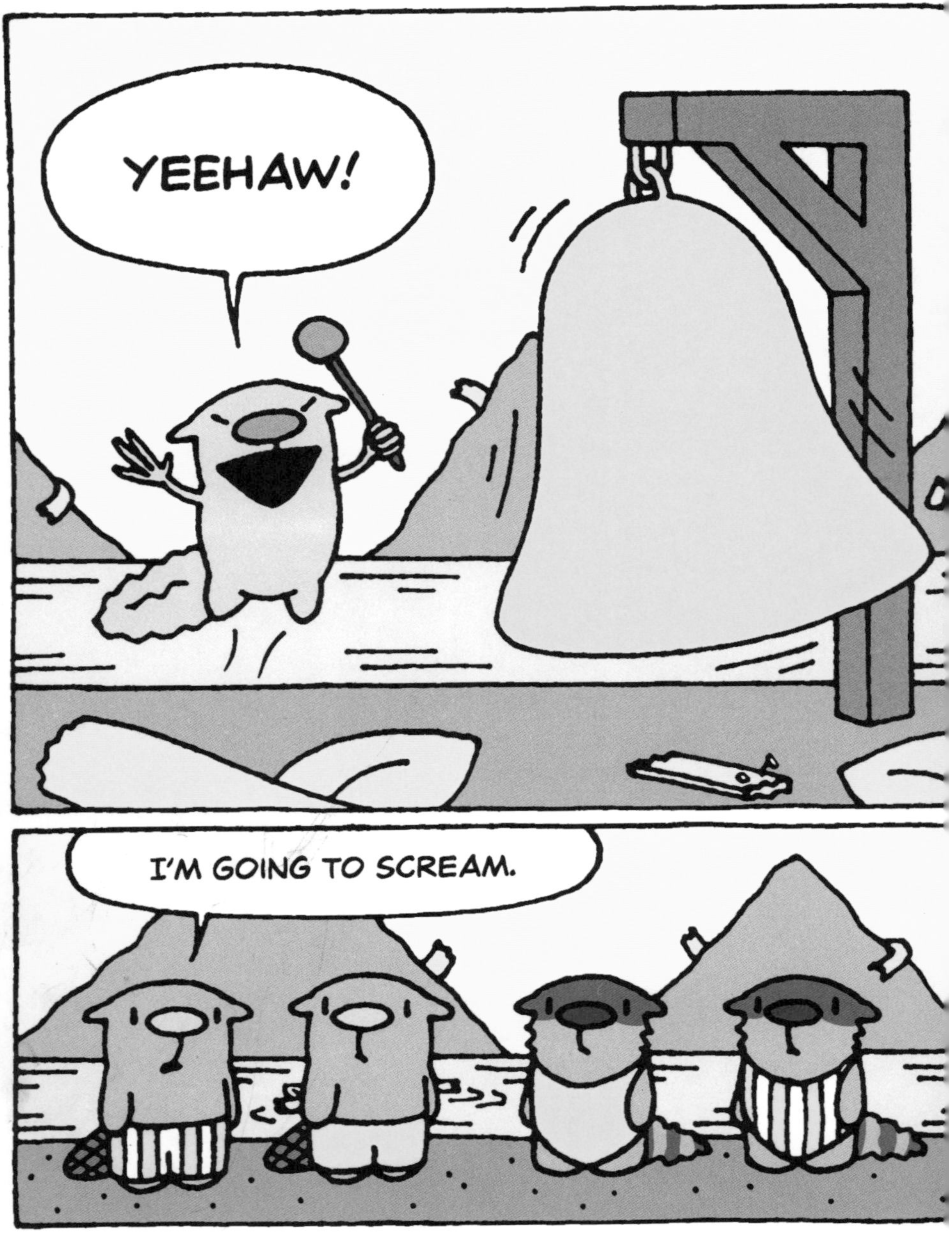
YEEHAW!
I'M GOING TO SCREAM.